RAVENSONG

Ravensong

A NOVEL

LEE MARACLE

PRESS GANG PUBLISHERS

VANCOUVER

The Publisher gratefully acknowledges financial assistance from the Canada
Council and the Cultural Services Branch, Province of British Columbia.

CANADIAN CATALOGUING IN PUBLICATION DATA

    Maracle, Lee, 1950-
      Ravensong

      ISBN 0-88974-044-5

      I. Title.
    PS8576.A6175R3 1993   C813'.54   C92-091582-5
    PR9199.3.M37R3 1993

First Printing May 1993
5 6 7 8 00 99 98 97

Editor for the press: Barbara Kuhne
Consulting editor: Vickie Sears
Cover illustration by Marianne Nicholson. *Dukwalha*, photographic collage.
Text and cover design by Valerie Speidel
Author photograph by Charmaine Peel
Typeset in Perpetua at The Typeworks
Printed on acid-free paper by Best Book Manufacturers Inc.
Printed and bound in Canada

Press Gang Publishers
101–225 East 17th Avenue
Vancouver, B.C.   V5V 1A6
Canada

*To all those women who fought the epidemic
when this country was not concerned with our health.*

RAVENSONG

Fʀᴏᴍ ᴛʜᴇ ᴅᴇᴘᴛʜs ᴏꜰ ᴛʜᴇ sᴏᴜɴᴅ Rᴀᴠᴇɴ sᴀɴɢ ᴀ ᴅᴇᴇᴘ wind song, melancholy green. Above, the water layered itself in stacks of still green, dark to light. The sound of Raven spiralled out from its small beginning in larger and larger concentric circles, gaining volume as it passed each successive layer of green. The song echoed the rolling motion of earth's centre, filtering itself through the last layer to reach outward to earth's shoreline above the deep. Wind changed direction, blowing the song toward cedar. Cedar picked up the tune, repeated the refrain, each lacey branch bending to echo ravensong. Cloud, seduced by the rustling of cedar, moved sensually to shore. The depth of the song intensified with the high-pitched refrain of cedar. Cloud rushed faster to the sound's centre. Cloud crashed on the hillside while Raven began to weep.

Below cedar a small girl sat. She watched for some time the wind playing with cloud. Above, she felt the presence of song in the movement of cedar's branches. She surrendered to movement, allowing the sound to spiral her into reverie. Her body began to float. Everything non-physical inside her sped up. The song played about with the images inside. She stared blankly at some indefinable spot while the river became the sea, the shoreline shifted to a beach she couldn't remember seeing, the little houses of today faded. In their place stood the bighouses of the past. Carved double-headed sea serpents guarded the entrance to the village of wolf clan.

Approaching the village from the sea was a tall ship, sails billowing in the wind. All activity in the village halted. The ship sent a small skiff out to greet the growing number of people gathering at the shoreline. There were no women in the boat. No women on the ship. The men scurried about, dragged out their largest feast bowls—huge carved containers, shaped much like their canoes. Young women were sent aboard the ship—fifty in all.

The child's body seized up, twisted itself into fetal position. The women were returned to the village. They became the first untouchable victims of disease. A new moral sensibility was required and the old culture died just a little after that. What had been the customary gratification of human need had brought death among the villagers. Never again would wolf women serve men in quite the same way. Fear, cold and thin, wove itself into Celia's self. It crowded itself between her moving cells. It silenced her. In a moment it was over. The weight of cloud augmented until the precious water threatened to cut loose from the dusty moorings held by sky. Celia returned to the village under the gathering cloud cover.

And then the rain came. Dismal and grey it whirled lightly, buffeted by erratic winds. The crowd fidgeted anxious for the man in front to hurry along and finish. It was unseemly the way it drizzled in erratic sprays around Old Nora. Stacey imagined seeing Nora screw up her nose the way Stacey did when the wind blew rain directly in her face. She couldn't have, she told herself: dead people don't screw up their faces. They may haunt people as spirits but their bodies are stock still.

Stacey looked around at the crowd. Nora had not been the delight of anyone's life, still the whole village had turned out. It was as if all the good citizens, relieved to hear of Nora's exit, had felt a twinge of conscience at her passing, so had spruced themselves up in decent black to bid her adieu. By now Nora's spirit was probably among the folks standing around watching the body, listening to the rhythmic drone of the priest. Probably grumbling right now, "Too wet for a damned funeral, I ain't going," Stacey told herself, hardly able to stifle a chuckle.

"Mommy, is this the Nora that was nosey?" Stacey couldn't help laughing. It was too true, too appropriate and said so innocently by Mary's girl. No one turned to frown at her. The two men standing on her left and right twisted their faces into pinched disapproval to mask their own amused response. All eyes looked down. Half the crowd coughed. Mary choked on her gasp, then told the little one to hush. The priest sped up his drone. Soon the body was being lowered into a hole.

"Too deep," Stacey's mom whispered softly. "Too deep to do the earth any good. Should've been cremated." Some old man murmured agreement. Everyone lined up to take their turn at shovelling dirt on the body. The line fell into place more or less organically, without the need for anyone to order them up. Stacey remembered being at other funerals—funerals full of passionate grief. Funerals of beloved old ones in which the grandchildren let go deep wailing sounds which seemed to come from the centre of the earth itself. Today there was only the feeling of relief and resignation.

She wondered why no one ever spoke at funerals until they had shovelled their share of dirt. The hollow thud rang eerily behind her own shovel-load, then she moved far from the grave, giving

Nora distance like everyone else did, and joined in the low murmuring about her passing. Between bits of wasted conversation around the fact that Nora had enjoyed a long and full life, Stacey couldn't help thinking just the opposite. Nora had lived long, but her life had been unreasonably empty. She had married some nondescript man who died before her children grew up; then she had put her back to the plow of feeding her young children whatever she could get her hands on. They matured after a fashion, left home and began families of their own. The two girls were still in the village, but the boys had long gone.

Nora never remarried. Well, maybe she wasn't totally single either. She always talked about how she had married her work, didn't need no man breathing down her neck, they weren't much good to her anyhow. Stacey was old enough to know what that last remark meant. It surprised her that her mind travelled along routes of imaging Nora's total disgust with the sex act. What a thing to be thinking about at a funeral. Nora seemed to whisper back at her, "Too young to know the truth about men." Stacey admonished Nora silently, "Can't you stop your nagging even now, Nora?" She thought she heard Nora laugh, deep and full.

The men were now seriously at the business of filling up the hole. No polite little shovel-loads. Muscles taut, unspeaking, they filled each shovel with sand and gravel and threw it earnestly in the direction of Nora's box. The rain was gaining on everyone. The priest hunched his shoulders, drew his head down into his neck, pointed his face at the earth, protected his Bible and made a run for his station wagon. A "woody" the boys called it, named for the wood panels on the side, Stacey imagined. She wondered why they were there. They didn't seem to serve any function. Engineers must have a wasteful sense of beauty she decided.

The woody chugged off, signalling everyone else that it was now polite to go. Stacey watched the men work for a few more minutes, entranced by their movement. No one missed a beat.

They bent backs, tightened their musculature, shovelled, rose and tossed in perfect rhythm. Each wore the same look of nonchalant confidence. Each relaxed into the shovelling, back glistening with sweat, staying completely focussed on the work. For Stacey the silent ritual of male physicality was captivating. She could not draw her eyes from the bodies of the men. Some small ray of light flickered in the pit of her stomach. Her thoughts began to sway and drift. Stella, very pregnant, waddled toward her, breaking up her reverie. The crowd drifted toward their cars. It was over, time to go.

Stacey jumped in with her cousins and a couple of aunts, carefully placing two little ones on her lap. Mary sat in the front holding her child who had blurted out at the gravesite. She was still stiff with shame at her daughter's remark. It had been so irreverent. Stacey wanted to tell Mary not to worry about what Alice had said, Nora hadn't minded. When people die they lose their attitude if it's a bad one and they gain in beauty if they are all right to begin with.

The rain sprayed delicate streaks across the window near where Stacey sat. She took another glance at the graveyard, whispering a thank you to herself. At least Nora was old. Although she doubted the assurances of everyone around her that Nora had lived a full life, Stacey knew why they had to say that to themselves. No one wanted to face the fact that life here at the edge of the world was empty for anyone.

Behind the car, in a cedar of magnificent elegance crow worried her wing. Stacey's last thought made Raven want to spit. Stacey might not be as bright as she had supposed, cedar sighed. Stacey will learn; if not Stacey, then one of her children. Be patient, she cautioned Raven. Crow cawed loudly. It annoyed her to think that cedar thought she knew something about the human spirit that Raven didn't recognize. Cedar sighed again and her branches brushed at the sky, subtle and serene—too serene for

Raven.

Change is serious business—gut-wrenching, really. With humans it is important to approach it with great intensity. Great storms alter earth, mature life, rid the world of the old, ushering in the new. Humans call it catastrophe. Just birth, Raven crowed. Human catastrophe is accompanied by tears and grief, exactly like the earth's, only the earth is less likely to be embittered by grief. Still, Raven was convinced that this catastrophe she planned to execute would finally wake the people up, drive them to white town to fix the mess over there. Cedar disagreed but had offered no alternative.

"Be patient," Raven repeated. "There isn't much time. These people are heading for the kind of disaster they may not survive. You, cedar, should think before you speak. You'll be the first to perish." Cedar shivered then wept in time with the rain.

Celia stood in the corner of the graveyard next to the fence which enclosed the cemetary, just a little offside the other children, who did not care to come too close to death. The fluttering hum of ravensong repeated itself inside her head. She drifted, floating into some confusing state of numb being in which the sounds she heard earlier whirred, disjointed from reality. Pictures floated up from her guts, hazy then sharpening with the growing intensity of her reverie. Odd pictures, disconnected at first, wheeled around in her mind, forming a web of knowing she was too young to understand. Somewhere else, in some other time men were digging, singing desperately, rushing through the digging, hurrying through the song. Men barely dressed in cedar bark wraps flew through the business of burying body after body. The digging kept speeding up, the urgency kept intensifying with the acceleration of the digging. A small circle of women whispered to one another, "Shorten the ceremony—we have no time."

Young women stepped forward to replace fallen men. The digging became frantic, with each increase in desperation the tears of mourning diminished until the digging and burying became sullen, automatic, without emotion. Another child's face came into view. A child staring blankly at a graveyard. Celia did not know the face was her grandmother's, surveying the wreckage of the first 'flu epidemic long ago. Celia's Gramma's brothers, sisters, aunts, uncles, cousins all lay beneath the ground. The sound of Raven died in the stillness. A woman approached Celia.

"Get away from there." She grabbed the child by the arm, jerking her loose from the fence. With that Celia returned to the present to watch Stacey. Raven sat peacefully on the fence not far from Celia, disappointed that this child had the courage to look while Stacey, who knew the others, refused to see.

Stacey had been to a funeral on the other side of the river, white town, her own villagers called it. She looked hard at the clothes of the villagers while her imagination recreated the attire of white town's funeral procession. Decent black was what everyone here wore. The others had worn black too, but there was something seductive about the black serge of the men's suits matching their patent leather shoes, and the women's wide-brimmed fancy veils and high-heeled shoes. They didn't grieve in quite the same way. The funeral she had attended was that of her only school chum's grandmother. Carol cried. She cried plain and simple, without much depth, no horror.

Stacey remembered with longing her own granny's death not too long ago—maybe two years. Stacey had grabbed Gramma's coffin, sunk her fingers into it, clinging futilely to the box while her voice had come up from some place deep inside her gut and let go a strange mix of terror, loss and grief that seemed so old, so huge. Her cousins had done the same. Gramma's daughters had all worn faces frantic and confused with the loss of the stabilizing rudder that Gramma had been. The air had been tense, filled with terrified anticipation of what life would be like without Gramma. Written on the faces of everyone at the funeral was the nagging suspicion that no one would recover from this.

Stacey's mother had been unable to stand alone. She had leaned heavily on Stacey's dad, the two of them staggering to the funeral site. The box was lowered so slowly and carefully, as though it were sacrilegious to hurry her away. The clouds had coloured the sky a deep charcoal. The air, thickened by the presence of dense overhanging cloud, had not satisfy Stacey's pumping lungs. Her mother had sobbed in the arms of Stacey's dad, who rocked her back and forth, tears streaming from his own face. Stacey, her brother and her sister had all slept together that night. The sound of wailing didn't seem to stop even after they slept. The burning had been better, less intense, without the cacophony of mixed emotions, especially the fear. In the kitchen after the burning, Stacey felt as though the daughters had all made a decision about their mother's death, a decision that eluded Stacey then as it did now.

Raven still sat on the fence enclosing the graveyard. She squawked. Stacey cast a look in her direction. She studied the raven, whose chin jutted straight out while she squawked. She had the feeling Raven was mocking her, bragging, telling her she wasn't very clever, scolding her for something she had missed about what had happened at her grandmother's funeral. It frustrated her not to understand what had happened at that funeral even now. She shook loose the memory of the burning, the change in her aunts and her mother. She hated the lack of clarity surrounding what had been decided by the women. Gramma's voice soothed her, "Don't worry child, it will come when you need to know." Stacey tossed the memory to a place of limbo in her mind. She decided to let it sit there until life imaged up some sort of answer.

Not everyone had cars in those days and the few who did had old wagons. No woodys, just plain old wagons. Each car was filled with car-less relations. It sure ain't like that in white town. Every car carries the family who owns it, not a relative more. Stacey wondered why. She let her mind drift around the habits of white town, their strange customs. It made better sense in English than in her own language. The lack of connectedness between white folks was difficult to express in her language. Most of the kids at school rarely saw their relatives. In fact, few had relatives that lived anywhere close enough to visit on any sort of regular basis. Who did they play with when they were small? she wondered.

Nora's voice interrupted her thoughts: "No use thinking about." It surprised Stacey that she had chosen Nora to address that question to. Nora's answers to questions were always laced with cynicism or despair. They were not all that useful. Still, she hadn't asked anyone else at the time. Like as not, Gramma would have given her an answer she could have sunk her teeth into.

The procession arrived at the muddy yard of the old hall. The village was extraordinarily proud of their little hall; just Stacey and the few others who attended school on the other side of the river knew it was nothing to be smug about. This was the West Coast, where salt hung thick and dense in the air, where wind, rain and age carved slashes of dull grey into the cedar siding of the hall's unpainted outer walls. Stairs led directly to doors without any sidewalks to preface them. The doors weren't real doors. They were concocted of plywood, like a lot of the doors to the raggedy houses in the village. The few windows were small and placed too high up to provide much light or view. Stacey knew why they were built that way—for child-proofing. An annoyance tugged at her. Indian kids are just like this here rain, a little wild and erratic. She bit back that thought, shoved it far away. It conjured too many memories of her ill-disciplined ways when she started going to white town schools, and the consequences she had had to pay for wild behaviour. While she didn't like her ill-discipline, she resented the consequences a great deal more. It was easier to just not think of it.

Death is strange. It begs change. It lurks about the heart, stubbornly straining memory. It conjures up images of whatever joy the deceased managed to bequeath the bereaved. When the body is finally laid to rest, the deceased's truth has been stretched to an image of virtue invented by the mourners. Death conjures these memories between tears. The conversation of the mourners always manages to wend its way toward these invented virtues of the dead.

"Nora could work. . . Best fisherman in the village. . . She could cut and gut half a dozen good-sized sockeye in no time. . . She was tireless." Even her constant fits of crankiness and her cynicism were recounted with laughter and some joy. The mourners weren't entirely wrong—everything they said was true. What had changed was their attitude toward Nora's character. Before the meal was over the villagers all agreed that Nora would be sorely missed. The words rolled around Stacey's ears sandwiched between her obsessive contrasting of their own dingy little hall to white town's community centres with lavish stone floors, elegant large windows, foyers and flowered walkways. It was unavoidable. Half of Stacey's life was spent across the river in the warm sanctuary of white town's evenly-heated institutions with their high ceilings; the other half was spent looking at the bedraggled single old hall that squatted stubbornly in the centre of her village.

Speaker got up to deliver words of encouragement over Nora's passing. It was not an emotion-packed speech. It was decent, but definitely not exciting. The cadence of his voice always moved Stacey. It quieted the children and brought low murmurs of agreement from the adults. In sweet language he recounted the life of Nora, her tireless wolf spirit. Self-reliant, she jogged steadily from the beginning of her childhood through motherhood, finally coming to rest this once. Stacey listened to him repeat, "It's how we are, *siem*. It is the pride of our women, *siem*. We are providers, mothers, tireless workers, *siem*. Wolf makes do with what is at hand, *siem*. There are no beggars among the wolf clan, siem." He moved to the history of her lineage, the great contributions some of her family had made. Wolf vision punctuated the generations that had contributed to the birth of Nora. Hardship was recounted in the context of Nora's clanswomen's heroism. Hardship was endured as though it really did build character and not just hasten life's journey to an early close.

The humming began again inside Celia. She watched Nora at work, then the face changed, rearranging itself into the faces of other women of long ago. She did not recognize the face of her great-grandmother working frenetically, obsessively, struggling to raise and feed a whole new family alongside her one surviving daughter. The images unnerved Celia. Nothing in them was recognizable. Adzes and fire reconstructed giant cedar into a boat; cedar vines became rope; bark became skirts, and roots shaped themselves into blankets. The child in her daydream worked equally frantically—tiredness was prohibited and the two of them, child and woman, denied fatigue while their bodies wasted themselves inside. Hard work tensed their faces, robbing them of their smiles. Hard work seemed to alienate the woman from the child. This picture was too much for Celia. It was far beyond her mind's ability to interpret safely. Her eyes awakened, let go frightened tears unseen by the room's occupants.

The rain drummed overhead now, keeping steady time with the Speaker's rhythm. Tears leaked through Stacey's eyes. Thin streams of water without any identifiable source of grief. Stacey didn't think about the absence of a source for her tears. Speaker always called them forth at the funeral feast. She watched the graceful movements of Speaker's body—almost womanly, so delicate were his gestures.

The atmosphere in the room shifted gently. Stacey's insides felt light, ethereal, impossibly whole. The lightness seemed to come from Speaker, travel inside everyone, pulling thin threads of ethereal being into a single spider web of spiritual oneness. Stacey felt invincible. The lightness danced, caressed unreachable places inside. Unreachable, without beginning or end, without name. It spiralled lazily, warming the cold places where doubt lingered. It curled about her musculature, resting somewhere in the pit of her stomach. As Speaker winded down, the lightness left. Her whole body felt content again.

As was his duty, Speaker invited anyone who chose to do so to come forward to speak. No one moved at first. He waited politely while the subtle ranking system fell into place. The elders of Nora's clan stared modestly at the floor, anxious not to exhibit too much pride by jumping up. The waiting was all so comfortable. It made Stacey want to get up to tell everyone how it is in white town. They don't like "dead air space," so they fill their whole world with needless chatter, even machine noises, as though they do not feel alive unless there is some racket going on. It wasn't her turn. She was neither old nor a clansman of Nora's, so she remained seated. Ella rose first. She slowly shuffled forward on her two canes. Two of her grandchildren leapt to her side, touching both her arms as they walked her to the front of the hall. At the front, Ella changed. Her voice lost its nearly ninety years of wear and tear. Her frame took on strength, her arms tensed, then relaxed. There was an almost youthful vigour in her delivery.

"Look around you," she urged. Everyone did. "See these children." The children all sat up straighter. "Pay attention to them. Life is precious—short. You are all visitors. These children are your guests. You own nothing but your kindness to them. Do not grieve those who have gone on. Turn your grief into kindness for the young." Her voice rose up at the end of each line as though there were no periods in her language, just pauses. The music in her voice sang sounds of gentle urging while her body stood stock still. After her speech was over she spoke in her own language. It was not a translation. There are no words to translate the significance of children or the sense of duty to family that mothers and fathers should have. The very word "child" in the language of the villagers conjures images of infinite grandchildren climbing mountains, heroically traversing thousands of years of the emotional entanglements life presents. The word rain images woman-earth, the tears of birth and endless care-giving. In English, rain is just water collected on dustballs too heavy to remain floating in the atmosphere. Stacey guessed that was why every speaker was certain everything sounded better in their own language.

She watched all the clan heads get up to deliver words to soothe the loss of Nora. Most struggled with the whole business of death from some philosophical perspective that eased the feelings of mortality funerals always bring up. They all carefully ordered themselves up in accordance with their rank and relationship to Nora, each speaker taking care not to repeat what others had said. After them a miscellaneous crew of speakers got up; last came the Christians, ever anxious to turn every bit of grief into a frantic search for Jesus.

"Find Jesus. . . " Stacey wondered why anyone could think he was lost. "Take Jesus into your heart," as though every mortal was some sort of spirit healer who could magically select Jesus from among the vast multitudes who must people the winds, and fuse him with their hearts. Poor Jesus. What a boring existence he must have if he has to listen to this for all eternity, Stacey quipped to herself. She wondered what this search had to do with his real life. Maybe when he was alive people from far away villages went off looking for him. . . No, couldn't be. . .

She stopped listening. She let her imagination re-traverse the journey of Nora's lineage. She watched her fish the river without a boat, alone under cover of darkness, one eye on her children, the other watching for the game warden while her hands worked her dip net, filling it with fish. She remembered how Nora had never been caught night fishing. Her kids huddled nearby under an old canvas she had lined with batting. She could sense someone coming. On the odd occasion when the fish and game wardens had come close to her fishing spot, she would straighten up, dart a look in the children's direction. Wordlessly, they ducked beneath the cover of the quilted tarp. All four would lay perfectly still and silent until Nora lifted the blanket. No one knew what Nora did during those moments when she was suspended between being caught and remaining undiscovered. Always she came home loaded with food fish, her children marching behind her.

Stacey cherished this memory of modest courage. Nora fished when the fish ran, regardless of the law outside herself. She was not interested in discussing her right to fish with anyone. She paid no attention to the men who rattled on about their right to fish— Aboriginal or otherwise. It wasn't relevant to her. Her children may have lacked clothing but they were never hungry—for Nora that was what mattered. Stacey longed for the simplicity of Nora's life, but her context was too different. She knew she could never be satisfied with village life now.

Celia sat next to Stacey, looking up at her periodically. In her hands she held an old rubber band which she stretched, relaxed and stretched repeatedly. When she wasn't looking at Stacey, she stared blankly at the busy work of her hands.

Raven laughed. She ruffled her feathers, curled her wings and roared. She had not thought about Stacey's innocence. Poor Stacey. She judged the world through a pair of glasses whose colours did not match reality. Stacey behaved as though she did not share the context of her clanswomen. Raven sighed deep and long. She sighed with the breath of someone who has been cut short of air. She sighed as though she were old, despairing of what to do with her sigh. She grew sightless and powerless in her pondering of Stacey. Stacey was lacking something. Raven knew

Stacey was lacking something but she knew not what.

Raven's insides jumped. Her feathers ruffled. Her body stilled. She wailed. It didn't help. Raven's wailing song was stilled by her own confusion. Raven could not power up the image she needed to end the drought which seemed to plague the people. It was a drought of thought. They had not retreated for some time to the place of sacred thought. Their thinking sat at the edges of their lives, rested on the periphery of the everyday, engrossed itself there and became shallow. Their thoughts avoided depth, lest struggle weary them. How to get the people to awaken was the dilemma which harassed Raven. If Raven could cut them loose from their obsessive focus on the now, deep thinking could be restored. Ah, Raven, Raven. . . black and sleek. . . black and sleek. . . Raven—black. . .

CHAPTER

2

THE RAIN CONTINUED FOR ANOTHER TWO WEEKS WITH-out let-up. It annoyed Stacey no end. Her arrival at school was al-ways more embarrassing on rainy days. Walking the half-mile from the village to white town in the rain soaked her clothes. Her hair lost whatever body she had been able to give it. Her ponytail became a single black streak down her back, her skirt stuck im-modestly to her skin, exposing short not quite lean legs. It wasn't cold but it made her wish for a Burberry, a pair of boots and an umbrella. The worst part was the squishy sound her canvas run-ners made as she walked along the long silent hallways between classes.

On regular days the students hustled past her without looking at her, but when it rained they all took surprised glances at her feet. She schlepped down the hall conscious of her feet, cursing her parents for having kids they could not afford. She cursed them for not going to school, she cursed them for continuing to live like her grandparents had, as though this world had not changed. It was 1954, for gawd's sake. Her dad still space-logged the hills of the reserve with a pair of damned Clydesdales while white town kids' folks discussed the burgeoning anti-colonial wars of Africa alongside the coming computer revolution. Her parents were caught in some strange time warp they refused to be freed of. She could hardly tolerate them on days like today. It was nothing so simple as a lack of education—her parents were both well versed in a whole different realm of learning. "No use thinking about it," the returning image of Nora told her. Nora's face whirled about the streaks of rain without acquiring any significance. She was just there, marching ahead of Stacey, floating really in the forefront of her musings as she hastened through the rain.

Although it always made her feel a little silly, she hunched up her shoulders the way the priest did on rainy days, hurrying to school with her neck drawn down turtle-like. It never helped but she seemed unable to stop trying to make this system work to keep her dry. Carol joined her just across the bridge. As ever, she offered the shelter of half her umbrella to Stacey. As always, Stacey refused. Carol chattered on about meaningless things— boys she liked, girls she didn't, bogus teachers—then she dropped the bombshell on Stacey.

"There's an epidemic coming—the Hong Kong 'flu." Stacey's head did a sharp one-eighty. She stopped.

"Christ." Frame after frame of the tubercular deaths of some ten years earlier jumped into view. They crowded the present, rendering her momentarily powerless. She had to struggle to stay conscious of Carol. Her mind wanted to focus on the significance of another epidemic.

"Whatsa matter?" Carol asked solicitously. She had already told Carol about the tubercular deaths which plagued her village for some thirty years some time back. This was the first tuberculosis-free year the village had had. Her body seized. It took some effort for it to go loose again. Death does not count in white town the same as it does in the village. The thought drifted about inside her mind and she let it roll around in her imagination for a while. She could see the meaning of death to the village. She watched the numbers terrify everyone. The loss was total. An untimely death meant everyone lost a family clown, an herbalist, a spirit healer or a philosopher who seemed to understand conduct, law and the connection of one family member to another. Every single person served the community, each one becoming a wedge of the family circle around which good health and well-being revolved. A missing person became a missing piece of the circle which could not be replaced.

White people didn't seem to live this way. No one individual was indispensible. Their parts didn't seem bonded to their whole. It wasn't that they didn't feel their people's losses, it was that their losses didn't seem to have much value. Carol couldn't seem to conceive of the threat an epidemic posed. Stacey just shook her head, frightened by how inessential the others were to one another. No wonder they can blithely watch us die, came into Stacey's mind. She fought for recovery, squeezing her thoughts small. The recovery tired her. A sliver of pale apathy replaced the fear. She thought about how this was her last year at school. Two months from graduation, now this. She would have to quit school if it came too soon. She watched her dreams of a teaching career draw to a close. For almost twelve years she had moved beyond the indignity of school—the insults, the loneliness, the silence of others who preferred the pretense of her non-existence—and buried herself in their strange books. She had wandered about in their crazy sense of self and logic, memorized passage after passage of seemingly meaningless information so she could go to the place where millions of books resided. She really wanted to shape a life for herself that was different from her parents' lives. All the sacrifices she had made in the interest of the dream mocked her. It wasn't just her either. Her mother had carefully socked away pennies, dimes and nickels to pay for the schooling Stacey dreamed about.

While her father logged, her mother had worked endless hours trying to make a little extra. She crossed the river every weekend to clean house or do laundry for wealthy white folks who paid her little. She sat up each night for hours under poor light knitting the wool socks white folks loved so much. The entire extended family had gotten involved. Every spare cent of every single one of Stacey's relatives had been put in jars for Stacey's dream. Even Uncle Ned, who now rarely came by, sent money to Stacey's mom for her education.

"Stacey likes school," so they all helped to gather free food from the hills behind the village in autumn to save having to buy groceries from white town.

"Running shoes are cheaper than oxfords," so they all trucked to school with wet feet half the year without complaint. Stacey felt sick. Her younger sister Celia had shouldered the heavy work that would normally have passed on to her during canning season because Stacey wanted to study. Moving pictures of Celia crowded her mind. Celia on a wooden chair heaving cauldrons of canned fruit back and forth, filling jars with boiled water, joking despite the huge effort canning took for her small body. Not this time. Stacey knew she couldn't get by without helping fight an epidemic. Her sense of family wouldn't allow her to leave it to everyone else.

"Are you all right?" Carol's question interrupted the sick feeling in her stomach, stopped it from bringing up her breakfast.

"Yeah," she managed. Carol changed the subject. It wasn't much relief but it did give her time to think, to calm down. She thought about the people in her village trying to determine who were the frailest, the most likely to succumb, who might survive, which of the younger women could be counted on to help. She measured her grades, calculated the likelihood of passing despite the crisis. The 'flu could not possibly last as long as the worst tuberculosis epidemic; besides, there are hospitals that we can all go to now. She breathed relief. It would not likely be as bad as all the other epidemics.

From far away in cedar's top Raven shrieked. This last remark was a specious one, a delusive one aimed at Stacey's preoccupation with realizing her educational future. The sound of Raven escaped Stacey, who struggled to enjoy her sense of relief. It would not be that bad, she kept saying to herself.

The class was restless at this time of year. More so because everyone was in the home stretch. In a couple of months it would all be over. Even the teacher seemed restless, anxious to get the works of them through the system and on to something new. Herb passed a note to Polly which she dropped. It didn't go by Mr. Jones. He strode down the aisle, calmly removed the note from her hand and read it out loud. The note contained explicit remarks about the evening before's tangle they had gotten into. Stacey blushed. Polly ran from the room while Herb and the rest of the boys laughed.

Stacey cringed at the laughter. Every time she heard someone being laughed at, the derisive laughter aimed at her during her school years revisited her. These days most of the male students who didn't care much for Indians just ignored her, but in the bathroom between classes the girls giggled and whispered, then fell silent whenever she came into the room. She always felt as though they had been talking about her. Today's laughter cut deep.

In the bathroom between classes the girls uttered mean remarks in low pious tones about Polly's lack of chastity. Stacey felt a tiny scream birth itself inside where healing light lived. She quieted it by focussing on Polly. She couldn't believe how small and mean they all were. So what if Polly had a little fun last night? Big deal! There was no use saying anything to these girls. As she watched the girls and listened to their words Stacey realized that the crime Polly committed had nothing to do with virtue. Half the girls condemning her had rolled around in parked cars themselves—it was getting caught that laid her out for condemnation. Stacey fought the urge to tell them they were all hypocrites. Polly is one of theirs, she told herself: "Nothing to do with me." She pushed back the desire to make the others account for themselves.

The sun broke sharp and clear the next day. It seared the edges of Polly's humiliation, which Stacey's mind still held in focus. At the same time the very clarity of the sun seemed to heat up her resistance to feeling anything for Polly. She hurried to school without bothering to take a look at the world around her. Clutching her arms to her chest she wrestled with Polly, trying hard to destroy the memory of her by scripting the day's work at school overtop the nagging memory of Polly.

Class returned to normal minus Polly. Stacey noticed a subtle veil of tension governing the behaviour of everyone in the room. It made the students look a little frail. She examined the hints of this frailty on the girls' faces, touching off a dialogue in her mind. It was a different sort of frailty than visited the faces of her fellow villagers. The frailty of her villagers stemmed from the hunger of the body; the frailty of white girls did not look physical. White people look like they would survive an epidemic quite well. What is it then? Why didn't Polly's shame at being caught possessing the worldly knowledge of sexual passion rest easy on their faces? It had nothing to do with them really. It was as though Polly's wickedness, her guilt, got tangled up with some guilt and shame of their own. It starched thin unpersuasive smiles on their faces, while just behind the smiles lingered a kind of nervous sadness.

Stacey knew that Maillardville's Catholic background still dominated their sense of morality, though the French language of the people had died. English had been their first language for some three generations, yet they clung stubbornly to cultural origins despite the language loss. She did not know a great deal about their faith but somewhere in its canons lust must be defined as terrible—sinful is the word the Christians at home would probably use. This lie of sin lived in their minds, while lust, the natural passions of heart, pushed up on their bodies. The reality of lust wants expression. The exorcism of it requires dispassionate repression. The conflict between expression/repression must underlie whatever was joggling up their need to condemn Polly, twisting their faces into paradoxical emotions. So far, the village Christians had not been too hard on anyone around the business of lust. This last thought soothed Stacey.

The tension over Polly grew thick. Stacey did not like the feel of it. The whispered indignation in the high school bathrooms seemed to ease the tightwire feeling in the air. At the same time, for some strange reason this very tightness brought colour to their faces that did not normally reside there. It was as though tension itself was a substitute for the sort of aliveness that ought to come with just being. Others walked about with heads down, falling into an uneasy quiet. The constricted reticence of these others seemed to expel aliveness the way it did for her people at home. These two things created a stormy churning in her stomach—butterflies of bewilderment flying meanly about. She ached for an end to her own internal disquiet. Stacey wondered if the insides of any of her classmates stormed about the way hers did.

It was Friday. Despite her mixed feelings for Polly, whose dreams had been so easily dashed because she was too frail to face shame, Stacey was glad. She and Carol had the unalterable habit of studying together on Friday night. It wasn't just the study Stacey liked, it was being at Carol's house she looked forward to. If she ignored the condescending presence of Carol's parents, being there was a delight. Everything about Carol's house sang comfort. The little pickets of the fence all standing straight at attention like little wooden tree people guarding the beauty of the manicured lawn contrasted sharply with the unadorned stone and sand of her yard. It wasn't even a yard. No flowers in neat stone-marked beds grew there. The plant life in her front yard consisted of the odd bit of comfrey interspersed with dandelions and pigweed. Only mint was cultivated by her mom—she carefully nurtured it. The scent of mint hovered lazily about her door entrance almost all year long. It had taken her years of composting and hauling dirt in buckets from little corners of the reserve to get it to grow. She watered the mint plants regularly. She rarely missed addressing the mint like old friends as she entered the house. It was the last of the old staples that the village still used on a regular basis. Only the odd family did not bother clutching at the delicate mint plants in front of their houses. Although Stacey couldn't imagine life without mint garnishing every dish, she resented the flowerless sandy yard of her home compared to the exquisite floral gardens and lawn patterns of white town. Mint looks like a weed. Cultivating it seemed so ridiculous.

No two yards were alike here. Each family conjured visions of their dream home, then laboured to realize the dream. It was the first sunny day after a long bout of rain. The hacking chug of push lawn mowers scudding about the neighborhood filled Stacey's ears. The backsides of women, their hands covered by real garden gloves, jutted up above the flowerbeds, while their arms worked to haul the weeds out from between the rows of flowers. Weeds. Comfrey root, dandelion, plantain and mullein were all being tossed of a heap to disappear in a strong black garbage bag out of sight from the public. As Stacey watched the women tossing the weeds to one side, for some reason she thought of Polly.

She saw Polly in her perfection being weeded from the ranks of her own, an unwanted dandelion. She wondered what magic medicine Polly hid inside her passionate self. A self that had inspired Herb to write the love note and risk being caught by giving it to her in class. Underneath this lay a question not fully formed which Stacey could not bring up far enough to ask: what powerlessness lay inside her magical self that killed Herb's loyalty when they were both caught? What drove Mr. Jones and her classmates to hold Polly alone to account for the actions of both her and Herb? Stacey moved directly past the question to scenes from her village. She knew they harvested weeds more or less indiscriminately, using them as crops to be eaten along with whatever store-bought food they could occasionally afford. Even while she resented the cultivation of mint, it struck her as pathetically funny that these people should invest so much time in throwing living creatures away when they were still perfectly good. She paid no attention to the paradox of emotions spawned inside her by her resentment toward her mother for nurturing weeds and her recognition of the pathos of white folks discarding wild food growing.

"We eat what them women are tossing," she said to Carol.

"Ohhh, you're kidding."

"I wouldn't kid you about a thing like that." Now it was Carol's turn to stop and stare in shock. It was the only thing Stacey had ever told her about her private life in the village. Stacey hadn't seen it before. It surprised her now that she could go to school with this person for twelve long years, spend half an hour every day walking to school and sauntering home again afterward, spend several hours together every Friday for four years, yet never mention anything about her life at home. She tried hard to remember some little detail she might have let go. There was none. Her school life and her home life were completely separate until now. Carol's response had been a ridiculous "ohhh." Stacey laughed. Carol joined her.

"I'm so gullible," Carol jerked out between bouts of laughter. Stacey roared all the harder because the joke was way over Carol's head. It excited her to think that Carol knew absolutely nothing about her, while Stacey knew Carol so well. Stacey re-looked at the two of them, comparing their lives. Carol took her whole life for granted and never once had to think about it. Unlike Nora, who fought hard not to think, Carol just didn't have the means to think. She had nothing to compare her life to. Everyone in white town ate store-bought food, throwing away the grocery items that grew wild in their yards the same as in the hills that rose above the town and the village. Aesthetic waste supplanted good sense and thrift in the care of their yards, while frantic saving coloured their consumption of food at dinner time. Because they hadn't the good sense to harvest what was in front of them, they had to tighten up on the amount of food they ate at dinner. The same mother who threw dandelion salad-makings away served stingy portions of food to her children at mealtimes, refusing them second helpings. It would have been amusing had it just been the plants these people threw away, but Polly was a young seductive woman whom no one wanted to see anymore.

Carol hadn't participated in the condemnation of Polly but she hadn't thought anything of it either. It seemed to fit into her neat little throw-away world. What was there for her to consider? Everything was as it should be.

"Hi girls," Mrs. Snowden sang out at the two of them, like she was both surprised and delighted they could drop by. Stacey felt a wave of endless cynicism stitching itself to her insides. For some reason Stacey could not help consigning these people's behaviour into some weird purgatory of helpless callousness. She read sinister motives into their every ordinary movement lately. This greeting seemed both false and fitting, almost characteristic of their world. Stacey knew most of the children of white town were transient visitors in the lives of their parents. Carol had told her she was expected to move out to fend for herself as soon as she turned eighteen. The enthusiasm now seemed so fake. It kept the two girls distanced from the woman.

Stacey rolled around Mrs. S.'s behaviour pattern trying to settle some fundamental truth about these people who had always confused her. The question, how could they be so dispassionate about one another? began to shape into answers in her mind. Since their children know they are temporary they must distance themselves from their parents long before the moment of departure, otherwise leaving would be too painful. In order to rationalize them being family they had to cover the lack of emotional intensity between them in a complex ritual of silly courtesy.

The entire table conversation at dinner was made of "Please pass" this, that or the other and "May I be excused," as though the children did not actually belong there. Stacey had never seen the children get down from the table to wander off without first asking for permission to do so. The children rarely spoke unless spoken to. The house did not belong to them. Today it all looked so weird. It was almost like they could just barely tolerate each other. This must have something to do with the gloom that surrounded Polly. She scolded herself: quit.

Stacey's dad came into view. The soft roundness of his face contrasted sharply with the hard, angular features of Mr. S. Her dad was quiet most of the time. It was the children who were noisy. She looked again and saw her mother take part in the children's playful banter. She saw her father for the first time give knowing glances to his wife. Her mother responded by teasing this or that one for the mess they always made. Stacey started to realize that these signals he gave her were consistent. As each child approached some pre-determined age they would evoke some look from her father that only her mother understood. The teasing was carved in a direction of self-discipline that somehow each of them had internalized, including herself. She wondered what the difference between the two men's behaviour was. Maybe her dad was just more subtle about ordering his wife around. She shoved that thought quickly out of her mind.

"You look lost in thought," Mrs. Snowden intervened, halting a question forming in Stacey's mind. It rose and sat somewhere in the air out of reach while she struggled to re-play in her mind what Mrs. Snowden had said. She needn't have; dead air space provoked another remark from Mrs. S.: "Are you worried about exams?"

"She won't likely have to write them, Mom," Carol answered for her. Mrs. S. purred, "That's nice." The subject exhausted itself without Stacey having to fully regain consciousnes.

"Did you know, Jack, that the Waltons are getting divorced?" she said, her voice flat. Mr. S's face got tight. Here it comes, Stacey thought, he's going to bawl her out for saying something in front of the children. Stacey stared down at her plate, waiting for it to pass. This happened occasionally at the Snowdens' on Friday. Stacey could not understand why Mrs. S. had no more rank in her own house than the children. Her father's looks nagged at her. The possibility that her mom's rank was based on her accurate reading of her father's subtle looks tried to take shape but Stacey shook the thought down, away from her consciousness.

"Cathleen. The children," Mr. S. chided. He stared down at his plate, his hand holding the dinner fork balanced as he fought to bring reason to his anger. Stacey could see him fight with anger but she couldn't figure out why. She watched him recover, plunging himself into the conversation with dispassionate vigour. Somehow the fork had helped him. Curious, Stacey picked up her own fork, balanced it on her hand exactly as she had seen Mr. S. do—it did anchor her somehow. Holding the fork in this way made it easier to contemplate his underlying thoughts: Mrs. S. had messed up and would likely do so again if he didn't get the conversation on track. "The company . . ."

Stacey knew she was safe to compare the scenario here with her life at home. There are no smells in white town homes lingering from the night before. The walls are all cleaned of the scents of yesterday's trace of life. At home, the stew from the night before lingered delicious during early morning breakfast, changing to traces of blackberry scent which hovered above the new meal's aroma until nightfall. Here, the occasional waft of perfume from Mrs. S. and the scent of Mr. S.'s shaving lotion sometimes caught Stacey's attention, but generally she felt like each meal she ate here on Friday was the first meal they had had in a long time.

"Is Richard worried about the potential man-hours lost by the coming 'flu?" Mrs. Snowden brought back Stacey's fear around the coming epidemic. A knot formed in her stomach. She had a hard time swallowing the piece of food she bit off. No one noticed. The room began to fill up with the strain of concentration that pretense requires.

"No, no, we have a substantial list of possible replacements. It should not inconvenience production whatsoever, Cathleen." His voice sounded chiding and condescending at the same time. Stacey thought she saw Mrs. S.'s eyebrow go up. Her chin poked itself out in an involuntary show of mild defiance. She recovered so quickly from this small piece of rebellion that it went by Mr. Snowden. Mrs. S. looked like she wanted to elaborate more; instead she stabbed mindlessly at her peas, pushing them around on her plate in a crazy half-circle. Stacey's knot subsided. A flash crossed over top the things she was seeing: Mrs. S. is making some kind of decision that hasn't anything to do with what's going on here! This confused Stacey more than it helped so she set it aside.

"Paper says lots of man-days will be lost," young Harvey, Carol's only brother, offered.

"Oh really," Mr. S. answered, as though Harvey were another man. Stacey looked from Mr. S. to Mrs. S. There is some kind of war going on here, she realized. Mrs. S.'s right eyebrow went up again, only this time her back straightened, stiffening itself as though her body suddenly realized she did not belong in this chair. Her lips pursed themselves tightly together. Mrs. S. stayed silent for the rest of the meal, while her husband and youngest child discussed the economic repercussions of the 'flu on his business. Stacey could not take the by-plays or the reality of this room any longer. Excusing herself she got up and headed down the familiar hallway upstairs. The hall looked unreasonably long. She didn't feel quite all there as she glided to the little room at the end.

In the bathroom she closed the door carefully, then leaned against it. What is going on inside my head? I am obsessed with living like these people but I can't stand them anymore. The house felt so empty, the bathroom so far away from what little life existed in the kitchen. It was the air, heavy and oppressive, she told herself. Fifteen pounds per square inch of pressure pounding at her because there was no human life to alleviate the feel of the pressure. She could hear Mrs. S.'s footsteps heading for the hall. Stacey must have been gone too long. She knew Mrs. S. was coming to see if everything was all right. Dichotomy. How could Mrs. S. be so solicitous about her being gone too long and so distant toward Carol? She quietly went to where the toilet was, flushed it, then washed her hands. The falsity of her actions shamed her but slightly. At the sound of the flush, the footsteps receded. Stacey cringed. She felt like a participant in the Snowden masquerade. A wave of fear passed through her. She told herself to get out of the Snowden house. For some strange reason she felt she needed a reason for leaving, but couldn't figure out a plausible one. In the confines of the lifeless house she couldn't comprehend that she needed no reason to leave. It was as though the thick weight of the air stilled her from imagining any right to leave without explanation.

Reluctantly, she returned to the table, forcing herself to wait a few polite minutes before she suggested going to study. Carol's response was so enthusiastic that Stacey felt guilty about her earlier desire to leave the house entirely. In Carol's bedroom they pored over the texts. Nothing would stick in Stacey's mind. She read the words but they slipped away almost as soon as her eyes recognized the shapes, and no meaning was translated to her mind. The words would not move from the typed surface to visuals she could hang onto.

"You really don't look well," Carol commented after a while. The phone rang. Carol reached for her extension, sure the call was for her. Stace saw her face change. Was it shock? She gave up trying to read Carol's face and waited for her to get off the phone. The scent of home kept invading her grip on reality. It pushed back the air-freshened scent in Carol's room. It squatted stubbornly in the corner of her consciousness while Carol stared at her in shock. Gently, as though to apologize for having overheard the conversation at the other end of the line, Carol put the receiver back on the phone.

"Polly killed herself," Carol whispered. Both girls retreated into the horrified silence of youth who dare not interpret the world of understanding specifically reserved for adults. This was too big. Stacey decided it was a good time to escape the entrapment she felt here in the Snowden house. Carol lay on the bed staring at the ceiling, just barely whispering farewell as Stacey left to return to her own world across the bridge.

The walk back passed by in a blur of pale grey. The cloud cover seemed to come alive, a dome of grey cool damp dancing about on the outer edges of her receding consciousness. Her body shut down, her mind denied the subtle numbing process taking place while it obsessively rolled about the death of Polly. Raven sat perched on a cottonwood just outside Carol's house, high above Stacey's head. Celia crouched under it, clutching her sides. She had been invaded by scenes of yesterday again and was trying to compress the scenes into dense balls of black nothingness.

Raven sighed relief, "Good move, go home." She whispered Polly's name to Stacey. "Polly . . . suicide . . . feel the life of Polly draining from her perfect body. Wander around Polly's insides, feel your way through decades, generations of lostness. Capture the moment, the precise minute in which the will to survive melts down to disappear in the millennia of futility her lineage has been. Discover her spirit, bent, then broken. Re-invent Polly, re-imagine her, hang onto the picture of perfect being letting go, spiralling down into shame. Picture the rootlessness she must feel.''

The words of Raven reaching Stacey were too complex for her to sort out. She had no idea where they were coming from so did not notice her little sister under the tree. Looking straight ahead she let the words toss themselves about in her mind in total disarray, images pulled up without order or meaning as she staggered toward home. The pictures skittered about between memory and consciousness without landing anywhere, until only the sound remained. Her legs, thickened by her confusion, weighted her walk home. Indiscernible noise flew at her, strident, then unclear, blending with the disorder of Raven's song of lament for Polly. Understanding stretched thin between her skin and the heaviness of her body, then sandwiched itself between the sharp strains bombarding her mind. Raven wept while Celia recovered. She fell in some fifty yards behind Stacey, following her big sister home.

The traffic hummed and swooshed by as Stacey tottered home. She should have said something to those girls in the school bathroom, she scolded herself between moments of contentious dissonance. She wanted to tell the teacher he was a brute. She wanted to cut the whole world of white town down the middle, surgically removing whatever it was that kept them rooted to their lifeless selves. She wanted to get beyond giving a shit about Polly, about Mrs. S., about their trussed-up yards, their empty houses full of crushing air. She wanted to go back to warn Carol she was headed for some nameless disaster, but the very namelessness of it discouraged her. The blood in her head pounded with the effort of trying to sort out Polly's suicide. Killed herself because they knew she had enjoyed her body's passion. It all seemed too absurd to be true. Stacey felt she must be missing some significant piece of information with which to solve the mad riddle running around in her mind.

Killed herself over lust. Stacey leaned against the fence in the middle of the bridge, grappling with her insides, trying hard to root herself to water's playful voice. Celia stopped not far away to hide in /the shadow of a telephone pole. Killed herself over lust. . . . splash, whish . . . killed . . . She fought to amplify the articulation of river's rush to sea in order to deaden the script set off inside by Polly's passing. Killed herself over lust. Splash . . . killed herself over . . . whish . . . killed herself. Water crashed against stone, ripping it from the embankment, growing louder until finally the internal quarrel was reduced to a repetitious whisper. She forced the last utterance from her mind. Finally the voice tormenting her fell flat and the river's chatter came up, filtered through what seemed to be a long tunnel. As the river's melody came closer, her legs gained strength. The weight of the air shifted away from her body. Stacey told herself that she couldn't afford to get this whacked-out over some white girl. The 'flu was coming. It would rip through her whole community barely noticed by the Snowdens or anyone else in white town. People would pinch out, "It's a shame," qualified by absolving remarks like, "Well, look at how they live. Three generations under one roof. It can't be healthy. Please pass the salt." The conversation retreated to the comfort zone of lost man-days, government ineptitude, or the failure of science to come up with some magical vaccine against any further inconvenience created by 'flu.

She knew old Dominic would do his best to ward off the danger epidemics posed to the village. He was a good healer with the sort of illnesses that were ancient, but he had not had much success with smallpox or tuberculosis—epidemics of recent times. Still, Stacey knew he would try. An inexplicable sadness washed over her. The stones below, worn smooth by water rushing over them to greet the sea, accentuated her sadness. They made her realize how small she felt just now.

Stacey looked up. Her little brother sat astride his bicycle looking at her, waiting for her to recover. Stacey could tell he was wondering what was wrong. She knew too that he would not intrude on her private moment on the bridge. He gave her a quizzical look, inviting her to confide in him. She had a right to her own intimate world. Young Jim would not violate her need for isolation. He assumed if Stacey wanted him to know she would tell him in her own sweet time. It made Stacey smile. She strolled over to where he sat motionless, ruffling his hair as they met. He grinned. She took quicker steps so that he would need less effort to keep his bike upright without looking clumsy.

"Some white girl in my class killed herself," she said flatly, like it was someone she had read about in the morning news and whom she didn't know. Young Jim drove on for a bit, reticent, then asked "How do you do that, kill your own self? Isn't some disease supposed to do it?" he added, to let her know he knew about the nature of dying by yourself. Stacey wasn't sure if he wanted to know how it was done in the practical sense of ways and means, or if he wanted some sort of conceptual answer that would solve the riddle of coming to a place of such cynicism that taking your life was the only path out. She opted for the first possibility because she had no idea of the why of the second. He accepted her answer: she had hung herself.

Celia watched them leave, then returned to her vigil behind the hall. She wanted to watch again the nightmare of tall ships she had had. Thin lines of fear etched her curiosity. She had hidden behind this hall a couple of times since she had first seen the ships. She let the rain fill her clothes with wet, drench her skin, while she ran the memory through her mind. She had no previous picture to assure her that this thing, this boat, existed. Who were the women? In her hand she clutched a branch the wind had cut loose from cedar's dress. She stared at it without really seeing it. Just as before, the visioning brought back the knot in her gut and a general feeling of paralysis. Numb, she was unaware that her armpits leaked or that the centre of her mind had birthed a small scream. At its birth the branch in her hand broke.

3

Daylight broke through Stacey's window like a gentle serenade singing sweet light to her lover, dark. The cedar outside her window danced. Through the moving leaves sun splashed spots on her bed in a rhythmic pattern of yellow splashes. In the dark folds between the leaves of the cedar just outside her room, Raven perched, studiously gazing at Stacey. It took great effort for Raven not to squawk at her to get her attention. She considered her plan to drive the people out of their houses. She knew they stayed confined to their villages for false reasons: segregation between the others and her own people had as much to do with how her own felt about the others, as it had to do with how the others felt about the villagers. Raven saw the future threatened by the parochial refusal of her own people to shape the future of their homeland. Somewhere in the fold between dark and light her people had given up, retreated to their houses in their raggedy villages and withdrawn into their imagined confinement. She had to drive them out, bring them across the bridge. She was beginning to doubt this was possible, however. Stacey, the child who had all the advantages of Dominic's and Nora's good sense and the knowledge of the others, was unable to hear Raven sing, no matter how obvious her song.

Raven considered the others: poor pale creatures who had forgotten their ways centuries before. She mused over their recounting of origins from the time Jesus was murdered. Parched throat, he had perished straddling sacred cedar in a land far from their own. They borrowed his spirit, his heroism, but did so in distorted fashion. Raven feared for young Stacey. Despite this she intended to carry on with her plan. These others had to be rooted to the soil of this land or all would be lost.

Cedar disagreed with Raven's plan—it was impossibly mean. How could Raven consider making the people sick? Still, cedar had no alternative. Everyone cudgelled themselves with the dilemma of getting the people out of the houses to immerse themselves in the transformation of the world of the others. For a hundred years now every attempt had met with little success. The ban against their ways had been lifted for four years now, still the people behaved as though they would have no part of the others' world. Their silence was accompanied by a strange paralysis.

Stacey alone moved about in the others' world. She moved about in it somewhat catatonically, as though she could not see through its façade of polite hierarchy. She seemed unable to get under it to expose it enough to find the key to its transformation. She was unable to say the words that might jar white town from its own sleep. "Be patient," cedar admonished Raven. "There isn't much time," Raven responded. "These people are heading for the kind of catastrophe we may not survive. You, cedar, should think before you speak. You will be the first to perish." Cedar shivered then wept in time with the rain. At the end of her weeping the rain stopped and would not resume again for some time.

Celia stayed sleeping. It was too soon to be awake but something had opened Stacey's eyes. Murmurs from the kitchen wafted through the curtain that served as her door. Movement, quick, decisive and sharp, muffled only by the care of the movers in the kitchen, followed the low murmurs. Something was up. The 'flu. It's here. She sat bolt upright just as her mother gave the curtain a jerk. For some reason the image of old Dominic, his medicine rattle shaking at dawn's light, jumped into view. The fantasy both startled and pained her. She pushed Dominic's apparition back.

"Good, you're awake. Get up. Ella's house has the 'flu." The realization that white people were right, they lived much too crowded in their tiny houses, hit her. Damn. Ella. Frail old Ella wouldn't make it. Stacey wanted to weep. She forced the tears back, swung into her clothes and dashed to the kitchen. She summoned what energy she had to focus on reality. Stay with the present. We have to try, she instructed herself.

"Sshh. You'll wake the dead." Her mother paused to look at her for a moment. Stacey had the feeling she saw deep regret peering through the lines of her face. Behind her eyes was some unknowable longing. Her mom seemed to consider sending her back to bed, then resigned herself to harnessing her daughter to the horrendous struggle ahead. There was no choice. They both knew they had no choice. Stacey lifted her eyebrows, shrugged, and her mother smiled.

"Take these pans. Go get the rubbing alcohol from the bathroom. Bring the comfrey and echinacea from the drying shed. Meet me at Ella's." With that her mother disappeared into the sweet dawn.

Last night's sun had set ripe red. The lines of light this morning were yellow. No cloud to fog the day. On her way out the door Stacey glanced at the clock—4:45. Outside dark faded gently into misty light. A rolling fog of golden yellow spilled from the eastern mountain edge to wend its way through the small spaces between tree and leaf, grass and bush. It leaned itself up against the eastern side of the few houses she could see. She could not help noticing how the yellow light softened the face of the village. No paint scratches could be seen on the aged unkempt homes. The gravel took on an ethereal life of its own. The overgrown grass captured the sun's colour in its pearl-drops of dew.

She wondered when was the last time she had been up at this hour. Ten years ago, the answer came easily. The world was so different then. There was a war—a world war. Benny, her mom's youngest brother, had enlisted. He wrote her mom dumbfounded letters in jerky English about the "ceremony" they had put him through. They had lined him up with three other Indians. They each held out their right hand, placed it reverently on a Bible, and swore allegiance to the King. Then this man in a grey uniform marched them to a desk where three neat piles of paper sat. He read them so fast that none of the three young men heard any-thing he said. They can talk really fast, Benny had said in the letter—so fast that all the words seemed like one long word. Then they signed next to lines marked with an X. Benny told them he could sign his name. The man in uniform laughed, saying the X was to mark the correct spot to put his name. Benny nodded sagely. He didn't like the man laughing at him like that but he never said or did anything about it. They all signed. Benny wanted to know what the papers meant. About two or three days later— Stacey couldn't remember now—Benny got "Canadian Natural-ization" papers. At the time no one in the village knew what that was.

Stacey found the whole scene kind of funny now. Momma trotted around from wise old sage to wise old sage with no luck, finally going to those who could read. They don't teach that kind of reading in school, most of them had muttered. Molly looked at it mumbling, "They only told us about Dick. I don't recognize any of these people here." Ida had really looked at the papers, then said kind of funny, "Ts Inklish ah-right." Momma knew that but she thanked Ida anyway. Robert had looked at the paper upside down, sideways, then straight up, but he couldn't make head or tail of it. Momma felt bad. Benny had asked what it meant. Momma was Benny's older sister. It was her responsibility to answer his question. She made up her mind to take a trip to town— not the local white town but Vancouver. Stacey had gone with her.

They rose at 4:30 in the morning. It had been early autumn. The chill morning air pierced the two of them. They trundled through the village over the bridge to white town to catch a bus. Stacey was only in first grade. She didn't quite know what a bus was, but Momma had done her best to describe it to her.

"It's kind of like a car, but longer and higher and with rows and rows of seats and lots more people in it." Her voice lost its soft monotone, as though the crisp air made it sound punchy.

"Like a truck with lotta people," Stacey pressed her.

"No, more like one of them cars," Momma said pointing at the priest's utility, "but much longer." Stacey stretched the Ford in her mind. The wheels looked too small to hold anything bigger than the wagon upright.

"Are we gonna crash, Momma?"

Stacey had been thrown off by her momma's laughter then but it made sense now. Little kids leave whole paragraphs out of their conversation, which the adult imagination has to fill in. She wondered what constructs had run around her mother's mind before her laughter stopped and she was able to assure Stacey they were not going to crash.

Stacey resorted to re-searching how the day had looked. Outside slivers of cloud had nestled against the skyline. The sun had painted the edges brilliant magenta while the centres faded to pink. An extravaganza of gorgeous happy colour for such a sad time of year, Stacey thought now. What leaves were left on the cottonwoods had been a tired old gold. They clung to the branches, desperately hanging onto life while the blood of the tree ground to a halt, ceasing to nourish them. Apples, ready for picking, clung to the branches of their trees. As they passed the apple trees Momma had mumbled, "Gotta get them kids to pick them things before they go to waste." Stacey had had to run all the way to town to keep up with her mom. The bus wasn't even there yet when they arrived. Stacey had asked why they had hurried so much if the bus wasn't even there. Momma didn't answer. She didn't look like she had even heard Stacey speak.

The bus was big. The smell of cowhide and diesel had made Stacey kind of sick. Some old white woman had given her candy. Momma thanked her, then when the old woman was out of sight, she cupped her hand underneath Stacey's mouth, giving a decisive but gentle tug at her lip. Stacey spit out the sweet-tasting thing without complaint. Later, on the way to the immigration office, Momma tossed it on the ground grumbling, "Crazy old woman feeding kids poison."

The white man in a grey uniform stood behind the counter with his arms outstretched, the tips of his fingers splayed across the counter like he was guarding some personal territory. Stacey recalled wondering why he wanted to guard a space so square, white and barren of the small things which transform a building into a home. No knick-knacks or baskets adorned the walls. There was just a giant photo of a lonely-looking man in a uniform decorated with bright medallions and gold braid. She now knew the lonely man to have been King George VI. At Momma's question the tone of the man's voice changed.

"It means he is a Naturalized Canadian." Stacey recognized the tone now. It was the same tone Mr. S. used on Mrs. S. when she messed up at the dinner table and let go some piece of news not fit for children to hear. It spoke of his attitude toward the two of them. Before him stood a dark woman dressed in plain cotton; a kerchief bound her head beginning at the arch of her eyebrows, hiding the lines of her forehead from view. The dress was frumpy, earth-coloured, too long and too plain. Momma was a bush baby. The man had secretly declared her unteachable even before he spoke. This unteachability inspired a disgust in him that oozed out through the pinched politeness of his voice. Momma felt this and flinched when he spoke, but she wanted to know what "Naturalized Canadian" meant, so she persisted, trying to ignore his attitude.

"What's that?" she asked. He sighed, shook his head in feigned disbelief, explaining the immigration process, the business of swearing allegiance to King and Crown, immigrating to Canada, voting privileges and so forth. Benny had been right, they spoke quickly, using words neither she nor her mom recognized. The man's words meant nothing to either of them but Momma thanked him anyway. On the way back, she had told Stacey that they would get the answer when it was time.

Stacey had all the medicine Momma had asked for, so she turned to leave. Fall is kind of funny. Stacey mused over the memory of that day long ago, remembering having glanced about, taking stock of the way the world looked. Even the noise from the earth had seemed sharper, anxious even. The trees had stood motionless in the half-light, but they didn't look calm, they seemed stiff, maybe even sad. Her recollection receded under the crunch of gravel underfoot. The fall of yesteryear faded effortlessly into today.

No lights twinkled at this hour except at Ella's house. She swung in the direction of the door. Just before entering she glanced back. The sun had come up whole and violent. The morning sky held the sun fully formed between the breasts of their ancestral mountains. No loose threads of vague colours trailed from the huge ball of yellow. It cast its light over the whole village already. Under its light she could see old Dominic, rattle in hand, returning from whatever place in the hills he had chosen to try urging the virus out of the village. He looked tired, terribly tired. For the first time, Stacey noticed how old he was. She shook her head sadly. She wanted to go over to Dominic and say something, but the words to comfort him escaped her. Instead Nora's voice came up, "No use thinking about." With that she moved to enter the house.

Momma would be mad. It had taken Stacey a long time to select the roots from the drying shed, collect all the pans and other things Momma had asked her to bring. Everyone inside Ella's was moving with even, sure gestures. There was a sense of urgency in the room. A couple of women from the village helped her mom tend to Ella while the others nursed the babies. Ella couldn't hold water down and she was incontinent.

"Should've called us earlier," Momma complained. It was the first genuine complaint Stacey had heard her momma utter. Involuntarily, Stacey's eyebrows went up. She looked askance at her mom. A look of challenge answered Stacey's face, but it didn't stay long.

"Drip the water into her mouth a drop at a time, Stacey." She did, pausing each time for the wretch she was sure would rack the old woman's body. Ella resisted the care and attention. She grabbed Stacey's hand. Stacey leaned forward to hear her whisper.

"What you going to save me for, have another baby?" Stacey cracked up. The women in the kitchen looked at Stacey. She repeated what Ella had said. They all laughed.

"Sure, why not, Ella. You probably still like trying." They were on a roll, ribbing Ella about her zeal for men. Ella chuckled between wretches, helping them along, making faces and raising her eyebrows every now and then. Someone was cooking. The scent of bacon and oatmeal wrapped itself around the laughter in the room. This was not going to be as bad as it had first seemed, Stacey thought.

The time flew by. Hour after hour Stacey dripped water into the woman while her mother swabbed her down. Others did the same for Ella's daughter and her three kids. Mary was the youngest of Ella's kids so her children weren't very old.

Stacey couldn't help studying Ella's face, comparing her with Old Nora. Despite the fact that Ella was the elder, she looked a great deal better than Nora had. 'Course Ella had not walked through life with a grim frown, biting her lips together all the time. It wasn't just that though. Ella's whole body was different, supple, fuller, almost inviting in her elder years.

"How old is Ella, Mom?"

"Eighty-eight," her mom answered. The medicine was ready. The dropper was filled with it instead of water. Kate, Momma's younger sister, took the dropper from Stacey's hand, motioning her to eat. She was grateful. Her wrist had begun to stiffen. Three hours of holding your hand out in the air carefully letting go fluid drop by drop was work.

"Bet you won't want to be a nurse for a living after this," Kate teased. They all laughed and rolled around that for a while, flogging it half to death. Stacey jumped into the fracas. She knew white women don't hold eyedroppers over 'flu patients; they have intravenous do the trick for them, but she liked the word-play and she knew they had no idea what went on in a hospital. So far, few who went there had ever returned. As a result, the whole village was convinced that hospitals were there to finish them off. Stacey thought this was a little unfair. She knew the villagers never sent anyone there unless there was nothing more they could do. Only the near-dead showed up on the doorsteps of the place. It annoyed the hospital staff no end. They tried to explain that the villagers should have come earlier, but no one was convinced. Since the hospital was going to kill them anyway, it made better sense to them to keep their loved ones near to them until the last minute.

"Did you ever find out what 'Naturalized Canadian' meant, Momma?" Her mom's spoon clattered slightly against the edge of the bowl. Her face betrayed no surprise, though, when she answered "No." She shovelled the food into her mouth a little faster. She was anxious. Stacey had constructed her question carefully so as not to mention Benny by name. Benny, poor stubborn Benny never returned from Europe. His bullet-torn body was interred there in a mass grave along with tens of thousands of other misguided young men who thought they were serving their country. Stacey knew her mother was nervous about her mentioning Benny by name. It wasn't good with the smell of death hovering just outside the door to call the spirits in. Benny might be lonely and could call Ella to join him. Dominic had conducted a ceremony for Benny to help him on his journey to the other world, but even Dominic had not been confident that Benny had heard. Her mother needn't have worried. Stacey wasn't sure anymore whether the mention of someone's name would lead to a new death, but she wasn't in a hurry to test out the theory.

"It means you're not an Indian anymore." The words crashed about the ears of the women. The women's voices fell dead, assassinated by Stacey's revelation. Even the air ceased to move. Kate rescued the situation with, "Just because an Irishman gets off a boat in Vancouver, it don't change his colour—he is still an Irishman. You can give our people all the papers in the world. It won't make us one of them." It relieved the stress. It was too ridiculous a notion to contemplate. Not an Indian. It was impossible. Stacey explained the legalities of Indian men signing up to "fight Fascism," the necessity of them having to naturalize to do so.

"What's Fascism?" Momma let it go with too much caution. Stacey told them it is when you don't have any rights anymore. They all looked at Stacey in disbelief.

"You mean our boys went to kill people they never met for that? Hell, we got that here. No one kills for that here!" Kate pronounced the sentiments of everyone in the room. Stacey hadn't thought about this when studying World War I and World War II, but it was true. The essence of Fascism applied to them all right, except the forced labour part, but the exclusion of Indians from working in the outside world started to look to Stacey like the flip side of the same coin. Her mother burned with shame. Benny had gone halfway 'round the world to kill young boys in a fight against something that he had not been willing to fight at home. She looked hard at Stacey. Year after year, day after day, the entire village barely managed to survive the endless prohibitions the government kept coming up with which seemed to be designed to starve them. Hunting and fishing were so diligently monitored and controlled by the game wardens that each family fell short of what they needed to get them through another year. Employers so rarely hired them that most of the villagers were convinced white people wanted them to die. Stacey couldn't help remembering her mother's response to her question some time back about the Depression.

"Hardly would have noticed it, 'cept a lot of white boys had to live like we do. They hopped off the box cars and came round the village looking for work in trade for room and board. Granny never turned a single one out without feeding him." Her words had come out tonelessly, cupped in an angry vessel which circled the tonelessness and betrayed her momma's rage. It still enraged her. "What had they done for us?" She threw her arms up at Stacey. "Their Depression would be over in no time. They'd all go back to work without a single mother's son among them ever returning to visit," Momma had argued with Gramma. "Indians are out of sight and out of mind to white men until they are in trouble," she had related to Stacey. Gramma owned the house then, so Stacey's mother had endured these white men in silence.

When Stacey asked what the boys were like, Momma had grunted, "Stupid and without shame." They couldn't do a single chore without endless instruction. They openly chased the young women, leering, smiling shamelessly, eyes all hopeful. They were disgusting about eating. If they didn't know what something was, they'd bellow out "What's this?" To Gramma's chagrin, Momma once answered, "What difference does it make?" Gramma answered patiently, "It's food, my son, eat up." "My son" still rang bitter in Momma's throat even as she repeated the story to Stacey.

"Shame on you, Momma," Raven now sighed from cedar's branch outside. Her sigh was deep and long. "The law, the law, must always be obeyed, particularly when it is difficult. Fortunate that you were raised by a woman who understood that. Perhaps her early death dulled your thinking. You of all people should know that upholding the law is personal—a thing of the spirit. It has nothing to do with the comfort or lack of it such laws provide. It has to do with the lasting sense of humanity the whole people feel from upholding the law and the good it brings to earth. Lawlessness, Momma, is heartless. Upholding it has nothing to do with the worthiness of others. To obey or disobey is not dependent upon their lawfulness or good character. Only your own spirit counts. You could have taken the time to teach these men when first I brought them here. You stood silent. Why would they return without reason?"

Raven shrieked one more time in a last bid for the attention of those in the room. None heard. She began to think her plan might not work. Doubt invaded Raven's spirit, her insides quivered slightly under the tensile thread of uncertainty. Hope shrunk inside Raven. She grew weary with the weight of its smallness. Then she left. It would be a long time before she returned in quite the same way.

CHAPTER

4

Momma sent Celia away from home until the epidemic was over. This hurt. Momma's look had told Celia there was no point in arguing with her. She wouldn't change her mind. The words bit into her gut even now as she crouched under the folds of the cedar, her bare feet touching dry dirt, unfeeling. The knot which came up at the sight of the tall ships returned. Immobilized, she choked on the knot as it moved up toward her throat. Eyes wet, she clutched her arms against her body, fighting for the words to soothe herself. Raven squawked from the fence. Even in her parched condition cedar managed to scratch out a comforting coo through her dry shredding skin.

Celia's body tightened, her hands clawed her knees. The knot moved into her stomach over the aching words, then edged its way up into the place air seems to come from. It filled her throat. Her mind lost itself in a tornado of frenetic images which refused to slow down to show themselves clearly. She lost her ability to hear. Cedar's warm tones perished under the squeeze of the heinous little beast invading Celia's body, scattering unmatched representations of today coupled with horrific pictures from the past in irrational patterns which hurt her mind. Raven's squawk was amplified in the windmill of pictures. Celia's eyes filled with senseless hate for the mocking pitch of Raven's voice.

"Shut up," she managed a low threat. Raven seemed surprised at first, then, offended, she ruffled her feathers, gave her wings a slap and flew off leaving Celia alone with her rage. It heated her insides to be this angry. It calmed her in some perverse manner for which she had no words. Her breathing restored itself on the wings of Raven's departure.

Inside Ella's, the work carried on with dogged determination, with only an occasional break in routine. A couple of times Ella's fever had risen out of control. She got delirious on these occasions. Once she went into convulsions. Both the delirium and the convulsions sped up the movement, deepening the intensity of feeling in the room in which they worked. Stacey felt herself free-fall into these moments of intense emotion. The eyes of the women spoke to each other wordlessly. They seemed to be communicating through looks. Although they had never battled this disease before, their looks seemed to be pre-understood, as though they had grown up always fighting disease together. A look and a nod from Kate instructed Stacey to refill the water bowl with cooler fluid. Momma raised her eyebrows in Kate's direction, which brought Kate to her side, dabbing Ella's forehead instead of her armpits. A sharp breath from Annie, Momma's youngest sister, forewarned of oncoming delirium and Stacey put more alcohol in the water. In these moments Stacey felt the power of clarity, but mainly it was dull repetition punctuated only by the occasional run of jokes.

Day left with Stacey hardly noticing. There weren't many windows in Ella's old house. All of them were high off the ground like in the church. Ella's long-gone man had built the house himself.

He had felled the trees, split the planks, erected it exactly in the style of their old bighouses, but with walled-off rooms. Above the windows on the east and west length of the house were lofts where the children had all slept. At the back, a double set of stairs led to the lofts. It was a big old house, warm in winter, cool in summer. Over the years he had managed to double-wall it, like white folks' homes, with plastering inside. The kitchen was spacious; its walls were lined with plenty of oak-trimmed cupboards, custom-made by Ella's Frank. Frank was handy with a hammer and saw. He had put his magic touch to a good many of the houses in the village during his time there. He had died during the peak of the tuberculosis epidemic. In the past couple of years the few who had become tubercular went down to Coqualeetza and returned. Stacey's mouth filled with bitter bile. Old useless Jake came to mind. He was the terror of Momma's generation. Mean, he terrorized his sad young wife in their home at the far end of the village. He stuck her in a hovel—barely better than a hobo's shack—refusing to let her visit anyone. He stayed drunk as often as he could; still his aging body held up. His wife, beautiful when she was young, walked with her head cast down and her shoulders bent. She reminded Stacey of some Dickensian waif. Why did he survive while Frank, hard-working and honest, perished? The world was full of unfairness; somehow the white man's God fitted in with the unfairness while Dominic's sense of the holy did not.

Frank hadn't known much about wiring so the lights in the house were minimal, but at least Ella had electricity; not everyone did. Because the windows didn't allow much sunshine to peer through, the light in the kitchen was always on. It was where the women put Ella's bed. Toward midnight her fever started to recede, by 2 AM she could hold down a cup of tea. Momma told Stacey to go to sleep, she had school tomorrow. Stacey breathed relief, relief for Ella and for herself. They sat around relaxing for a few minutes before Stacey left. Kate snuggled comfortably in her chair, cast a look at Stacey, then asked her how old she was.

"Seventeen," she answered.

"What! And no kids, no man!" Stacey blushed. She wished she had taken her mom's advice sooner and gone home to sleep. It never failed—adults in her family behaved as though only young people endured the kind of hormone rises which translate into the need for sexual liaisons. They constantly ribbed the youth about this or that boyfriend or girlfriend: "Where were you last weekend? Saw that young Charlie boy drifting in your direction, didn't look like he was going to help chop wood either." Or else they behaved as though having no children was such a sad and sorry deprivation for young women. For most of her village kinswomen, no kids meant no adult entertainment, no boyfriend. Thus far, Stacey had managed to put off the young men without too much difficulty. She wasn't interested in any of them. She never wanted to have to say that to her family so she used her schooling as a defence. Momma rose to her defence now, harrumphing that she would have plenty of time for children when she finished school. It almost closed the conversation, but Kate was not to be put off.

"What you going to do with all that book learning? There aren't any jobs to be had here that need it." Momma flinched. She did not like the new bend this conversation was taking. She had put off thinking about the end of the road in Stacey's education. An involuntary need to tell Kate she was awfully cheeky prying into Stacey's motives like that swole up. She shoved it back. It was too dangerous to push back on the rights of the women to rear each other's children. What Kate said was true, but Momma preferred to dream of Stacey coming home after university to teach her fellow villagers, thus altering the course of their history forever. It was an unlikely dream but it kept Stacey's mom from killing hope in dribs and drabs the way her sister Kate did. Momma felt trapped. She was not entitled to shut Kate up or to shape Stacey's dreams to match her own. She closed her eyes hoping the moment would just die. Stacey surprised them all. She knew exactly what she was going to do. Indian Affairs had a new policy—Indian Day Schools on reserve. She wanted to start her own school, right here in the village. It was the first time her mother had ever heard Stacey articulate her future, and it matched perfectly with what she felt were her own impossible dreams.

"What's this?" Stacey carefully explained the business of Indian Day Schools. Their reserve had enough kids to qualify for one and she would graduate four years after high school eligible to run the school. The women all talked at once, firing questions at her. What are they going to do with the residential schools? Will there be proper religious instruction? What about the learning, will it be the same as what white kids get? The question about religious instruction took her by surprise. Her mother was virulently anti-Christian. Stacey had assumed that her momma's friends were too. Kate alone had snorted at this question. They carried on badgering Stacey for news about her plans till nearly school time. The possibility that the horror of residential school and shipping out their children would be over excited them all. Stacey left them there still marvelling at her mom's wisdom in making her stay in school. Stacey wanted to build a school here, of all places.

She was dog tired, her arm hurt like hell now, but her spirits were up. Future. Stacey's plans stretched out down the road past the seasonal time markers everyone else still used. Plans to the villagers meant getting ready for the sockeye run, saving up for a hunting rifle or counting the number of new jars the women would need for canning next year. No one planned four years down the road—certainly anything beyond survival was never given a moment's thought. Now here, right in their own village was a seventeen-year-old girl bright enough to think ahead four years into the future. It was so amazing to them.

Stacey didn't bother going home. She turned from the village toward school. It was exactly one month from the day Polly had hung herself. Stacey still couldn't pass by the bridge without thinking about it. She hated the way Polly used up space in her mind. Today was worse than usual. She finally decided that it was the conundrum of suicide itself she couldn't let go of, not Polly's death. What sort of bend in your personal spirit did you have to have to end your life?

She stopped at the bridge to look down into the water. The little river was really just a creek. There were a few straggly fish getting the rush on the rest of the sockeye that would come up river some time later. They made her think of the Adams River run and the falls swimmer had to leap to get to the spawning grounds. She had gone there with her parents only once, but the memory of it stood out in her mind clear and strong.

Swimmer leapt, followed by her mate, who flipped his tail up, trying to heave her up and over the falls. Co-ordination was everything. It took the two a number of tries to get it so that she went over. Then it was his turn. He pooled about in an intense circle underneath the falls, gathering speed and strength for the near-impossible jump. After a few minutes of circling, he made a frantic leap at the falls. They threw him back; he hit a rock, gashing his side. Again, he swam frantically in circles in the pool, accelerating his speed to make another run. For two hours, swimmer's mate dashed at the falls, until finally by some miracle he cleared them. His mate had treaded water in the shadows of the bank patiently waiting for him.

Stacey's neck hurt with the tension of watching the fish. Only when the mate cleared the falls did she relax. Her dad whispered reverent words of encouragement to swimmer's mate, then turned to Stacey's brother and said, "And that's how our men feel about Creation." He turned to leave. Stacey had spent days turning over the image of the two fish in her mind. Both fish knew they would die. The end of the trail for them began with the need to procreate. Their courage was augmented by the brutal truth that there was nothing in it for either of them but death. That is how our men feel about Creation, she had repeated over to herself, shivering. The mate had first heaved swimmer, heavy with eggs, over the falls, then focussed on the task of getting himself over. He would have died trying, Stacey knew. She also knew swimmer would have waited in the shadows until death claimed her as well. The shiver froze Stacey's insides. Both children knew their father expected no less of them. This picture rooted Stacey to a sense of duty she could not explain, but she suspected that white folks lacked this sensibility.

Maybe that was it. Maybe some white people had no roots in the creative process, so could not imagine being that devoted to staying alive. If you have only yourself as a start and end point, life becomes a pretence at continuum. White folks, even her friend Carol, all seemed to be so rudderless. Because of that the kids at school seemed to suffer from a kind of frantic desperation. Maybe no roots was the problem.

The memory of the Adams River run faded. Stacey realized she was late. She would have to serve a detention. She decided she wouldn't serve it. She already knew she didn't have to write her exams, and the provincials were already over. Why bother?

Celia had been watching Stacey with some interest. She was curious about Stacey's vigil at the bridge. Although the hurt over being sent away shrank in size, it never quite disappeared. Still, there were advantages in not being there during the illness. She did not have to work, and she got to watch from a distance the effect all this work had on Stacey. She was vaguely aware that her understanding of Stacey lacked intimacy, but had no words to articulate her awareness. As Stacey's back disappeared over the arc of the bridge she realized Stacey was already a woman when

Celia first began to remember her. It made her want to cry. Her memories were restricted to Stacey taking care of her. Now that Celia was seven, there was no need for Stacey to dress her, feed her or entertain her. Celia was bewildered by her need to cry. She kept watching Stacey from under the shade of cedar near the fence where Raven used to like perching herself.

As the days went by Celia maintained her scrutiny of her sister while Stacey worked with the women inside the houses as they battled the illness. She imagined Stacey's character unfolding under the light of the fight against the 'flu. Stacey's devotion to healing the fallen didn't seem to fit Celia's previous understanding of her. There was something inside Stacey that Celia could not yet know about. Cedar brushed Celia's cheek with her lower branch, a soft caress from the smooth side of her needles, changing the direction of her thinking. She got up to look for someone to play with.

CHAPTER

5

Old Dominic had been by a week earlier. He had talked about the kind of summer it was going to be—long and hot. So far today was hot and the twenty-four hours at Ella's had made it seem long. Owl had been by delivering messages of death-doom, which Stacey already knew was on its way. She didn't marvel at the message owl had delivered to old Dominic. She knew he had a way of talking to animals. Dominic had also mentioned that Celia was spending much time alone in cedar's shadows, but the family had paid little attention to it. Stacey gave his comments no thought. She did consider asking Dominic about Polly. She had wondered if he could conceive of Polly's life in the outside world. She decided he couldn't. His soft slow ways, his character gentled by his conduct could not envision the meanness of the outside world.

After Dominic left Stacey had gone to bed determined to settle this business of Polly, wanting to rid herself of the space Polly's death took up in her mind. In the dark her analytic thoughts unfolded in shallow logic. Stacey took care to leave her heart out of her final examination of Polly's death. Polly had perished under the dome of arrogant insecurity her people had erected for her. They set up morals no human could possibly follow, then established a judgement system based not on whether or not you actually lived within the moral code, but whether or not you could deceive people into thinking you lived by this code. "Discretion," they called it. In Dominic's mind morality was irrelevant. What lived inside was a set of laws which were to be obeyed at all times regardless of the circumstances. His belief in their ways kept him on a trail of gentle social affection. He would not believe that anyone could consider that committing an indiscretion was worse than committing a crime. Lawlessness, over-indulgence and deception were just other words for thievery—only what you stole was the sacred right of others to choose based on clear knowledge. Deception robbed the hearts of others. Now Polly's life lay stilled in some graveyard because she had dared to be indiscrete. They weren't very likable people, Stacey decided.

As Stacey neared the bridge the sound of shushing cedar branches stopped her. Celia was under the tree. She looked odd there. Each time a branch shushed by in front of her, her face disappeared for a second. She didn't seem to be watching anything. Stacey cocked her head, told herself she'd be late for school and then turned away from her sister. Cedar danced gently, singing soft words of encouragement to Stacey's receding back.

"Come back, see how Celia hurts." Raven squawked at cedar to mind her own business. Cedar sighed. She knew Stacey's heart was hardening. Stacey had not seen the ache on Celia's face. Cedar strained to call Stacey's attention to Celia. Stacey could comfort Celia, ease her pain, but Stacey hadn't heard cedar's call. "Only the truly kind can ever be free," she breathed quietly.

Cedar knew only the truly kind possess the courage to get under a thing to study it thoroughly. A membrane of purposefulness around the future was closing Stacey's heart to Celia's present desperation. Kindness had a long-distance meaning for Stacey. Looking became not just a matter of seeing what's there, but seeing what could be. She was not yet seasoned enough in this kind of seeing to realize she had to keep the present clear to know how today becomes tomorrow for everyone.

"Hard-hearted people lack the will to labour to see from more than one angle. The membrane becomes layered with disappointment; the feeling that labouring to see isn't worth it stops you from seeking further than your own future." Cedar's words drifted out along the edges of the river to the sea without reaching Stacey's ears.

Soon the school was upon her. The classes were already in session. The hall looked particularly dismal, rigid in the absence of human bodies. In the half-light it achieved an empty kind of gloom. Four more years of this kind of institution, then it would all be over. She didn't want much to do with them after school was finished; despite her penchant for the things they owned, their ways seemed a little schizophrenic. She wanted the things without their ways dangling from them.

The class was all abuzz. The teacher was talking about the current scandal that rocked the province: the Hong Kong 'flu epidemic, the crowded hospitals and the unwillingness of white doctors to treat Indians on reserve. There were articles posted on the wall. Stacey particularly hated this class. It tended to bring to the surface the endless bigotry of both teacher and students. The teacher shot her a look.

"You're late," she said.

"Yes," Stacey answered quietly, placing her books on her desk.

"You will have to serve a detention if you have no excuse."

"I have an excuse. I watched the fish swim upstream and thought about Polly," she answered.

"Not good enough," her teacher replied.

"It will have to do because I am not serving the detention." All hell broke loose. The teacher's voice took on an almost hysterical quality at the challenge to her authority. The students were abuzz with Stacey's surprising nerve. Whispers and shuffling reached Stacey, dream-like and surreal.

"You will serve your detention or the principal will deal with you," the teacher snapped.

"Did you want me to see him now?" she asked quietly.

"As you wish." Stacey got up to leave. The principal's office was austere, sterile. The blue door hiding the inside was closed. The secretary asked her what she would like. Stacey tried to think of an answer. What would she like? I would very much like to be transported to another time, another place, she thought.

"Nothing, really. I was sent here."

Mrs. Cramer was taken aback. It wasn't the usual answer. But then, this was not a usual student; she was from the other side of the river. Mrs. Cramer called Mr. Johnson on the phone.

"The Indian girl from across the river is here to see you." He was a serious man. He had always taken the time to mention to Stacey that he knew she was doing well with her studies, asking how her family was, but he had never been too pushy about being friendly. Stacey liked him. It was always difficult for her to meet white men who inspired her to like them. The paradox of their general unlikability coming up against the odd good one confused her sometimes. She was aware that this man could disrupt her life, destroy her dreams if she told him the truth. She opted for honesty anyway.

"What have we done?" Why people with power over your life say "we" when they clearly mean "you" was beyond Stacey.

" 'We'? Well, I have decided I won't serve any late detentions for a while. . . . sir. I was up all night with old Ella, dripping tea into her old bones, trying to save her from dying. I stopped by the river to watch the fish go upstream to spawn. It revived me in a crazy kind of way to think that these little fishes your people claim cannot think could be so passionate about life that they would risk death to procreate, even though at the end of spawning they are all sure to die. At the same time people like Polly choose not to live over a little thing like sex."

His mouth dropped for just a second, like he couldn't believe what she had said. He closed it quickly, reddening slightly. He looked at her. The power Mr. Johnson wielded was illusory to Stacey, yet she knew he was full of this power. It was the power to decide people's futures but without the wisdom needed to guide them to their future realization. He scared her, yet she had stilled his voice so easily. She saw Dominic's image behind him. Dominic had no authority to make decisions for anyone, yet no one made decisions without consulting him. He had an enormous sense of the external world. Just beyond Mr. Johnson's stilled body she could see Dominic, hear him talking about the coming African revolt, how Black people would shed the first blood that would change the world forever, including her own. That was his response when she consulted him about whether or not she should go to university to return to teach school on the reserve.

"The world needs a combined wisdom, not just one knowledge or another, but all knowledge should be joined. Human oneness, that's our way." He had drawn deeply on his pipe, letting the smoke go so tenderly it filled the last words with reverence. It was a clear show of support from old Dominic. What he respected about the knowledge these people had to offer was beyond Stacey. It didn't matter. He was behind her; that was what counted. It dawned on her now that by her simple faith in Dominic she had given him power. Her acceptance of his sense of truth was the source of his power. Stacey had just relieved Mr. Johnson of his authority over her. She felt light, airy, like she did in the village hall back home when Speaker spoke. The stripping of Mr. Johnson's authority made Stacey his equal; the possibility of oneness with him opened up old fears.

"Sit down," he said, coughing slightly. He began in his usual father-principal voice, which got in the way of achieving any understanding. She persuaded him that nothing but a crisis ever kept her from school before, and that she would likely be late more than just this once during the 'flu epidemic. He argued his authority in the eyes of the teacher; if he let her "get away" with this the other students would take advantage of it. She argued that he ought to imagine every student and every situation on its own merit and not try to box-car everyone into the same package. He agreed with her intellectual sense of the individual, but not to treating students as individuals. It was too much work, went off in Stacey's mind. He did not have to say so for Stacey to know this was what he meant. She chuckled about the notion white folks have that others are lazy while they busy themselves with idiot's work to avoid the difficult task of working everything out anew.

"You have the power to cut my dreams short and expel me," she said simply, "but I will not serve any detentions for lateness." She spoke tonelessly and rose to leave.

"You have not been dismissed," he retorted sharply, to which she raised her eyebrows, smiled condescendingly and replied "That's true" as she closed the door.

She became a conundrum in the school. She was issued detention after detention. Two detentions for not showing up for the first detention, until she owed more detentions than there were school days left. Mr. Johnson couldn't relinquish his now vaporous pretence of power, yet he could not bring himself to expel her. Stacey didn't bother to think much about the hold she seemed to have on Mr. Johnson; she just carried on as she pleased.

Meanwhile the scandal of the 'flu epidemic was causing quite a stir in North Vancouver, not far from Maillardville. Some amazingly articulate Indians were stepping forward arguing human rights, justice and equality. The arguments were undeniable.

Somehow, though, this business of equal rights for Indians was rife with challenge to white folks. Stacey read the newspapers over and over again, trying to figure out just where the problem with these people lay. Under the shabby arguments about hospitals being full and doctors already overworked lay an unspoken assumption: white folks were more deserving of medical care. There is a hierarchy to care. In some odd way Stacey could not figure out how this assumption was connected to their very view of the nature of their authority. It continued to baffle her. Something was not being said here.

Stacey became the little town's personal challenge. She was not as articulate as the North Van chiefs. She made no effort to translate the neglect of her village into political challenges to white authority. This relieved Mr. Johnson. It stopped him from condemning her. In fact, Stacey did not seem to expect white folks to take care of any of the villagers. What was disturbing for Mr. Johnson was her quiet faith in herself, her absolute belief that she had the right to disobey a direct command from him without raising any kind of fuss about it.

The students looked at her differently now. Actually, it was more like they saw her for the first time. Until then, outside of Carol, no one seemed to notice her. A few of them hurled insults and racial epithets at her, whispered "cleutch" as she passed them in the hallway, but mostly she was ignored. Now her invisibility at school was greatly disturbed by her resistance. She wasn't sure she liked it.

She stood at her locker choosing which books to bring home, trying to decide whether or not she would realistically be able to study. Three more houses had been struck. She hated seeing the illness ravaging the community at home, while she sat comfortably here in class, mulling over much nonsense. This business of ancient history butted up against her current reality all took on a ridiculous quality. She had been standing there for some time because the hall was quiet. Finally, she put her books back. She would miss them. Despite the ridiculousness of exploring the pyramids of ancient civilizations she found them fascinating. Reading about them seemed somehow to alter the immensity of the world. Just knowing that the world was not so completely white relieved her. Even science, with its man-puffing character, was interesting.

"Not going to bother studying?" She recognized the male voice behind her as Steve's, the class intellectual. He invariably had the most to say in Current Events class.

"No," she answered softly as she turned to leave. He swung in beside her. She felt uncomfortable. Not once had she ever given any boy a signal that she could be interested in him. His voice made her aware that she was especially indifferent to white boys. She did not wish to end up like her cousin Shelly. Shelly had married one of them a few years back. She had to move off the reserve—not an Indian anymore. After a few years and a couple of kids, he left her. The last Stacey heard was that "welfare" had her kids and she was living down on the skids in Vancouver. Best to leave well enough alone.

Stacey had over the past few years developed a practiced look of boredom around all young men who expressed any desire for her. Putting up invisible walls, she called it. It worked for the most part, not because boys were sensitive enough to recognize a clear "No," but because none had been keen enough to work hard at stirring up her desire.

"Well, I guess I won't offer to carry your books home then." She didn't answer.

"I heard about your set-to with old Johnson." Stacey wanted to laugh. She knew how disrespectful white kids could be behind their teachers' backs, but she also knew the disrespect was false. Not one of them ever seriously challenged the authority of teachers. Probably because they dreamed of owning that sort of authority one day. Steve was an ideal candidate for the steady acquisition of such authority. He was bright, ambitious, confident, white and male. Of all those attributes, Stacey knew the last two counted most.

"He said you gave him quite a lesson in sociology."

"What's that?"

"The study of social relations—power, really. He also said you were upset about Polly."

"Not really. She isn't one of mine. I just found it hard to believe that anyone would kill themselves because everyone knew you had gotten laid." She bristled at the ease with which she pushed up this lie.

"It wasn't just that," he answered. She got the feeling she had plunged herself into hot water. The heat of it made swimming to shore with any vigour difficult. She was not going to be able to extricate herself from this conversation very easily. What sort of authority held her to this conversation with Steve was not clear to her. He was her peer, he posed no threat—at least he had no control over her dreams. So why couldn't she tell him to leave her be? Shelly's ghost returned. She was on the skids, not exactly what she had dreamed about when she got married. She had dreamed of white picket fences, manicured lawns and flower beds. She married someone like Steve, a nice white boy going somewhere. Now she had no children, no home and no dreams. What sort of authority is that?

"She had a miserable home life," Steve continued, recounting the violence in Polly's family home. "No girl who is loved at home would go out and look for sex." Stacey laughed.

"What's so funny?"

She realized he was not kidding. One thing white people say about us is true, Stacey told herself: we have no illusions that virginal behaviour is virtuous. People love, laugh and have babies. Half the women on the reserve had no piece of paper to prove their husband's devotion or to legitimize their right to mother children, but no one dared to refer to them as anything but so-and-so's wife or somebody's mother. Where do you begin telling someone their world is not the only one?

"You love your point of view so much that you make sweeping pronouncements about everyone else's behaviour," Stacey replied.

Steve casually fell in beside her, as though to walk her home—much to Stacey's annoyance. Since he hadn't asked to join her, there was nothing to say no to. What sort of authority is that, she wondered? She didn't have to talk to him. She could tell him she didn't want him on her side of the river, that he didn't belong there. Instead, she just didn't look at him. Maybe he would get the hint. He didn't. The air was vaporous and the sun rippled through into waves of discernible heat. The blacktop on the road was soft in spots where it was relatively new. The humidity made the heat indefinably oppressive, like Steve's presence.

"What makes you think that?" he had said some time ago. Now he was repeating his question using different words. She could see Carol out in her yard next to her mother pulling weeds. Comfrey root lay all about the ground around them. Momma was worried last night about running out. Stacey swung into Carol's yard, Steve at her heels.

"Can I have those?" she asked, pointing at the weeds.

"Those?" Mrs. S. asked, incredulous.

"Yeah," she answered.

"What on earth for?" to which Stacey offered no response. Mrs. S. shrugged, said sure and told Carol to fill up the bag.

"Do you have any more?"

"Well sure, they are out in the back, but they are mixed up with a lot of other weeds, dear." Mrs. S.'s face got a little strained at Stacey's insistence on the weeds, but she was mildly apprehensive about the answer she might get if she queried Stacey again about what she needed them for, so she kept quiet. Stacey read the look on Mrs. S.'s face, accurately guessing what was going on in her mind. She decided to leave everything unsaid.

"I'll sort them out," she said heading for the back.

"Here, dear, take these gloves." Stacey smiled as she took them. She didn't want to tell Mrs. S. that half the joy of gardening was feeling black earth between your fingers and that she wouldn't likely use the gloves unless Mrs. S. followed her to make sure she did. She didn't say anything. On the way back she considered the huge gulf of silence between them.

Polly used to look at her in class every once in a while, smiling shyly. Neither had ever spoken to the other, but Polly's smile had invited her to some sort of relationship Stacey had never picked up on. Now she wondered what the absence of words between herself and Mrs. S. had in common with the lack of communication between Polly and herself. On top of this, Nora's stubborn presence repeated "No use thinking about" over and over in perfect time with the rhythm of her weed-pulling.

Steve helped her sort out the weeds. He easily picked up on the difference between the roots. For some reason she started telling him what each plant was and what the villagers used them for. He didn't seem surprised.

"Does Mrs. S. know what you use them for?"

"No," she said laughing, then she got a little nervous. It was the first time she had taken any white boy into her confidence. Steve did not seemed to be affected by her taking him into her confidence. She had lurched onto dangerous territory without realizing it. The lizard, the lizard that the people let in, unwittingly, had just crawled through the doorway. Is that how it happened with Shelly? Old Dominic had talked about the lizard with her just last fall, the green lizard of human disruption we innocently let inside our houses. After he wreaks havoc in our lives we wonder why we let him in in the first place. Dominic had been talking about the old snake who abused his wife. She had let him in.

"Maybe humans want oneness with all humans," he answered in response to his unspoken question. "Maybe the spirit is our source of affection and it gets trapped inside the layers of poison we are fed in the course of our lives." Stacey realized now that Dominic had been warning her, not explaining Madeline's attachment to her vicious husband.

There were two bags of plants by the time they finished sorting. She dropped the gloves around front, thanking Mrs. S., who still looked bewildered by her desire for the weeds. Steve carried one of the bags as they left.

At the ramparts to the bridge she hesitated. The arc rose before her, separate from the ramp, representing power in its curve toward the sky. She couldn't see the other side clearly. The arc seemed to hang there all by itself. Somehow this arc and Steve shared the same sort of invisible power. This frightened her a little. For the first time she was challenged by what her people would say to her bringing home a young man who was clearly not one of them.

As she edged her way up the arc of the bridge she wanted to stop. She could feel her legs growing reluctant to pass without taking a look at the fish, but Steve might get the impression she wanted to extend his time with her. A crazy argument began inside. She wanted to laugh at herself. She could just tell him, "Look, I am not interested." White boys always have a response which is designed to save their pride by assaulting yours. Something like "Who said I was interested?" would likely fall from his mouth, bringing up shame to hers. She could hear him say that he just wanted to talk. She would then feel ashamed of misreading his intentions. She would end up feeling like a fool for deluding herself into thinking that a boy could be romantically inclined toward her. Christ, I don't like them, Stacey mulled. If they aren't busy being obnoxious to us, they are busy putting us in awkward situations.

At the far side of the bridge a half-dozen crows argued over carrion. They sputtered, squawked and raised a huge ruckus. One of them, neck stretched, seemed to be aiming his indignation at her. The disarray and the squabbling wanted to find some significant connection to the past month's events, but she chased the thought away. Disarray. She felt it much more strongly now as flashes of argument ran around her mind. If she stopped for her habitual private vigil he might ask what she was doing. He might disturb the peace of the vigil, contaminate its peaceful nature by disrupting its privacy. Why should she not carry on as always, despite his presence? She never invited him along. If he said anything, so what. She didn't have to answer him. She knew she would, though; it would be rude not to.

She decided to turn the lizard out at the arc of the bridge. She put her hand out, grabbed for the bag, then said goodbye. He handed it to her. He had the same look on his face that Mr. Johnson had had. The slave had just given an order to the master, which made him an ex-master. Neither man knew what it was to be an ex-master, so both were confused and hurt.

Stacey's eye caught sight of Raven, who seemed to be laughing at her. The tree she perched in swayed slightly as Raven tilted her head to one side, cackling. Stacey's attention was drawn to the possibility of Raven having some design on her. She shook her head, convincing herself it was just a crow—a foolish crow. Raven straightened up, thrust her head forward, letting go an indignant shriek. Stacey flinched, focussed her gaze on the rest of the trek home, and thought no more about Raven.

CHAPTER

6

"OH GOOD, WHERE DID YOU GET THEM?"

"White folks pull them from their gardens and throw them away."

"Really? you're kidding. Oh, you can't fool me, my girl," her mother let go a hearty laugh. Stacey just looked at her—the laughter stopped dead in its tracks unfinished.

"You aren't kidding are you?"

"No," and her mom shook her head back and forth.

"I will never understand them people. Help me tie these up." They set to work tying the comfrey in bundles, then hanging them over the old McClary woodstove. Stacey chuckled softly: her mother could move from profound realization to the mundane so easily. Young Jim jumped up to go outside to split kindling, after which he brought it in. In a very short time he had a reasonable fire going.

"Well, this should make the heat unbearable." They all laughed. Stacey felt a sudden affection for her brother. She remembered her annoyance at him when he decided he was too manly to go berry picking with the women and kids. Men. They all want to eat but they do next to nothing to go get the food, she had complained to her mother. Momma had reminded her she never had to chop wood, hunt or swing the dip-net or haul the canning kettle. She answered "Well, why can't I?" to which her mother said, "You can, you just don't."

She tossed this memory around while she tied up the roots. Women in this family do one kind of work, men do a different type. It wasn't a matter of being allowed to do this or that, it was choice born of some ancient string of normal action. Custom, she thought. Custom must be some sort of invisible policeman channelling everyone through a tube of unspoken discipline. Can there ever be a truly free world? The question dogged her while her imagination unravelled pictures of Old Nora, who chose to fish, hunt and space logs rather than remarry. No one treated it as odd, but there seemed to be an unsaid absence of total acceptance of eccentric Old Nora. Was that it? Did the fact that Old Nora broke rank limit the level of acceptance?

One of her daughters was just like her, except she never married. She had two kids from unknown men and she set about to raise them just as her mother had raised her. After some time, she brought a friend home—a white woman. The two of them still lived in Old Nora's house. No one wondered about their relationship except Jake, the old snake who beat his wife. Every now and then he staggered to their doorstep to holler "queers" at them, to which Nora responded with a rifle shot. Then he staggered home and all would be peaceful again.

"I think I am obsessed with dead people," Stacey muttered.

"That's because you are young," her mother answered, grunting and sighing from the effort of stretching to tie the bundles.

"What do you mean?"

"Well, young people can't imagine death. So they keep looking at the lives of the dead. I don't know why—maybe Dominic does, or Ella. They just do. Pass me some more string."

Everything was simple for her mom. The why of things didn't seem to matter. It was "I have no idea why, pass the string." Stacey wondered where she got her obsession with wanting to know why, when all around her the villagers seemed content with passing string, tying bundles or wiping babies' noses. Her mother had not come home with her last night and Stacey knew Momma had not slept today. The litheness of her faded with the night. Around her eyes large dark circles had formed. Her hair hung loose. She had not had time to fix it this morning. Stacey saw the age on her mother's face for the first time.

"How old are you, Mom?"

"Twenty years older than you," she answered. Only thirty-seven and already there were streaks of grey in the hair which framed the little crow-tracks around her eyes. Stacey wanted to ask why she had not had children after Celia, but didn't dare. It wasn't her business. Stacey remembered her sister Rosa was consumed by tuberculosis, then Celia came along and that was it. She thought something must have happened. She felt a chuckle rise in her throat—here she was again wondering why.

"What?" Momma asked. She was having trouble stretching to the right height to hang the bundles and Stacey offered to change places. She had two inches on her mother. This made her mom laugh. Stacey was relieved her mom took this as the answer to her question. No sooner were they finished than Momma was ready to go out the door. Two more houses had been struck. She cautioned Young Jim to stay home.

Stacey looked out after her mom, pondering the reticence of the village: like a living organism, it seemed to be gripped in a major sulk. No children hung about in little groups or scampered about. The whole village was quarantined. No one visited. No one went outside. They hid from each other in isolation. A handful of fearless women moved about to tend the sick. Momma fashioned masks for those who worked with the fallen. Young women spent hours washing out the homes. Old Dominic kept conducting ceremonies in secrecy each night, hoping to cast out the disease. He regularly sent cougars and bears back to the hilltop homes they peopled, but he couldn't speak the language of this virus. It was too small for him to see, he said. Nevertheless he kept trying.

Stacey watched Momma walk halfway to Martha's house, then she stopped to talk to the white woman coming this way. "German Judy" everyone called her. They talked a little while, then parted. German Judy headed toward their house. Stacey opened the door before she got to the stairs.

"Come on in," Stacey said, smiling. Stacey was aware her smile was a practiced one. She gave Judy tea, then patiently waited for her to state her business.

"We need aspirin. It'll reduce the fever."

"We need a lot of things, Judy," Stacey answered. "We need flower beds, lawns, pictures for our walls. We need a steady supply of good food and while we're dreaming up our needs why don't we dream up getting the white man off our back." Her tirade took her aback. What brought that on? Stacey could not keep the razor's edge out of her voice. Where did the sharp edge come from?

Judy smiled, answering, "My church is prepared to buy whatever aspirin is needed, but we have to pick it up. Your mom said you'd come along."

"Sure." Judy had a car. They both swung into it, not speaking at first. Stacey realized she hadn't ever spoken to Judy before. In fact, no one spoke to her or bothered to include her in the gossip much. She wondered why this woman chose to live in a village that virtually ignored her. She was white. No one we know, Stacey told herself. Judy hadn't once intruded on the space of any of the villagers. She went to work and returned home to Rena's,

accepting the village's silence about her presence. She didn't belong but no one said that.

"Where do you work, Judy?"

"I'm a legal secretary." She answered what, not where, but
Stacey didn't care. Why she felt she wanted to talk to this woman
was beyond her, but it felt kind of pleasant being in her car asking
questions, even if she answered questions the way Nora's daughter Rena did—monosyllabically. It dawned on Stacey that maybe
her segregation from the village was self-imposed and comfortable for her.

"I see you on the bridge almost every day staring at the water,"
Judy said easily.

"I watch the fish and think about Polly." The honesty of this
remark stunned her slightly. She tried hard to remember telling
white people the truth; outside of today with Steve she couldn't
remember being this honest. Too late now to take it back.

"Is that the girl who killed herself?"

"Yeah."

"Her mother is trying to divorce her father. He beats her
pretty regular, but it isn't enough reason to divorce. Women have
such a hard time sometimes," Judy said with a sigh. Stacey mar-
velled at the ease with which this rolled off Judy's tongue. White
folks have so little problem being intimate. She half wondered
why.

"You can't get divorced if your husband beats you?" Stacey
couldn't believe this one. The law office Judy works in must deal
with the divorces in white town, she thought. Her cousin Tessa's
divorce rolled around overtop the rest of her thoughts. Tessa had
simply heaved her husband's clothes out the door and him after it.
Now she was remarried. Well, it wasn't exactly the same. Neither
of her marriages had been sanctioned by the law.

"Why doesn't she just leave?"

Judy sighed. It had the same sound as the one she could hear herself make when the words are too many and there is a small place of doubt inside that tells you it all doesn't make much sense anyway. She looked out at the row of houses, wondering about the horrors that go on inside in perfect secrecy. Not being able to divorce was frightening. Judy explained a whole bunch of stuff about property, how women can't live in their homes if their husbands don't let them have the house.

"Don't let them have the house? What in the world gives him the right to a woman's house?" Stacey interrupted. Judy explained that men owned the property in white society, to which Stacey retorted, "Who gave them the houses?" Judy's shoulders tightened. "Sorry, finish your story," Stacey apologized for interrupting. In the end what struck her about Judy's narrative was the lack of support in the white community for Polly's mom. Where was the family in all this? There were no support systems for white women, not among their relatives or in their communities or in law. No wonder Polly killed herself. Until now Stacey had bagged white men and women in the same sack. White women started to look different. Stacey felt a little uneasy about this.

They arrived at the church, got the aspirin and left. To Stacey's surprise, it was reasonably painless accepting the charity of the United Church. Judy held the key to some of Stacey's questions about Polly. She made up her mind to visit her and Rena so she could unravel this business of suicide. Judy drove her right to the doorstep.

"Thanks, Judy," to which Judy mumbled a smile and drove off. For the next ten days, Stacey would not be at school. The sickness drove through the community like a miserable tornado. It ripped into the children, ravaging the young and the old. Death knocked on almost every door. Each night the owl, plaintive and sad, called a new name. Old Dominic eventually wearied with the futility of his nightly efforts to drive the sickness home. Momma began to tire, her breathing changed from its usual steady rhythm. Stacey

noticed that sometimes she seemed to stop breathing for long periods, sighing deeply when she resumed. Momma hauled herself
along on sheer grit alone. It aged her to continue to roll up her
sleeves tending the sick. Nora's daughter Martha recovered and
leapt into the fracas. Even Judy and Rena rolled their sleeves up,
donned Momma's make-shift masks and joined the other women
who felt it was their duty to try to save the community.

Stacey too felt this duty. She pulled at her youthful strength
night after night. She heated water in canning kettles, hauled
wood and dripped drop after drop of cooling tea down the throats
of resisting patients. The dehydration of the babies was swift.
Among the old the resistance to waging another fight with death
was strong. In tears one night the women admitted the illness was
too big—the old had to be left in the interest of the babies.

From outside the window Celia heard this. She froze, felt the
same knot come back that she had first felt under the tree when
Momma sent her away. The knot stopped her breathing again,
stilled her voice. She couldn't hear the rest of the conversation.
Her mind kept repeating, What would it take for them to let me
die? Her body folded into a crouch, her breath shortened, threatening to stop, her torso grew cold with fear. What would it
take? . . .

Stacey dared to suggest they try intravenous—makeshift intravenous of their own. Her mom agreed to go to the hospital to look
at the patients who had the 'flu. Two of the women said their boys
would steal the plasma and the equipment needed to save their
villagers. Another meeting was held. They decided to tell them
yes, but take the supplies from Vancouver, not here. They did.
German Judy drove them. They came back with loads of glucose,
saline solution and the necessary instructions. Stacey had to go to
the library with German Judy to figure out what the instructions
meant. They hooked up the sickest to the three intravenous appa-
ratuses. Like a miracle it worked. No dehydration.

The boys went after more glucose, saline and another apparatus. Within days those treated with intravenous recovered. It made the women furious that they should be left in total ignorance about how easily the disease could be treated. It infuriated even German Judy. Martha's oldest daughter made up her mind to be a nurse. If nothing else, they received a gift in Rilla's commitment to becoming a nurse so that never again would their community be ravaged by a curable disease.

Dominic still went out each morning with his rattle; each time he came back looking more fatigued than ever. The flesh of his face sagged, weighted with disappointment and inadequacy. The sun intensified with the building intensity of the epidemic. The wind whispered an eerie deep sound which Stacey imagined to be the song of Raven calling transformation from the deep, but no rain came. Dominic mumbled something about it one morning as he passed. He took to mumbling to himself on his daily morning trek. It unnerved Stacey. She did not want to witness him becoming senile. Stacey could hardly look at him after a while.

It had been days since she and her mother began rising at sunrise to leave the house, returning late at night. A terrible tiredness stole into Stacey's body—a fogginess of the body overcame her, making it difficult for her mind to get much cooperation from her body. Her agility was waning. The skin outside transformed itself into an unfeeling sack barely holding her parts together. She and her mother lost their ability to pay attention to their family. They failed to see the illness which crept inside their house, invading Stacey's father. He kept up his funeral duties late into the night as the sickness took its toll. Each day they lost two relatives. Two graves had to be dug. The men swung themselves into battle, digging, digging, digging, while the women fought the illness. Her father returned home one night exhausted beyond words. He rested for a short time, then left them. He decided to stay with the young men camped outside. They nodded to one another, parting without entertaining any thoughts about his well-being.

In the hushed solitude of night's blackness the 'flu carried away her father and Dominic. Like an odd pair of twins, neither had said anything about their illness. No one noticed they were not well. The two men perished as unassumingly as they had lived. Momma's grief was immeasurable. She sang her wailing song night and day while Young Jim, tiny and manly, rocked her. Stacey sang with her. Women came to join her—singing, trying to help her expel her terrible grief. At the gravesite she clutched at the coffin screaming, "No, not my Jim," over and over again. The entire village came out, including the old snake who beat his wife. They waited hour after hour until finally, exhausted, Momma let go.

If Stacey had no idea how to take her father's death, Dominic's confused her more. After the double funeral she took herself over to her house. The village felt empty—oddly freed of an intangible hold Dominic had had on it. The freedom did not feel right; an augustness had died with him. Nora's cynical sentiments grew large between the gaps created by Dominic's absence. Both Stacey's father and Dominic had had a kind of invisibility in life that became obvious only in death. Their presence, the hugeness of them, only presented itself in their absence.

In the house during the evening after the funeral Stacey realized how much her father had filled the home with surety. He had referred to everything as "Your mother's"... "your mother's home," "your mother's meat," "your mother's children," but his presence owned every nook and cranny, filling it with an uncanny comfort. In his absence the house became large and empty, dark and cold. Her mother, usually raucous and cheeky, was now small, dangerously fragile, subdued and lacking in courage. Stacey feared she too would sicken and die.

That was about when Ned came home. Celia had returned shortly before Ned. She was a shadowy figure to Stacey, who hardly noticed her presence or absence. Outside of amusing her little sister, not much existed between them. Stacey was about to leave for a long time. Celia moved about the house avoiding much contact with her at first. Stacey was caught up in cementing herself to Momma, eating up whatever time they had left without much concern for Celia. She failed to notice the watchful eyes of Celia.

"Death is transformative," Raven said to earth from the depths of the ocean. The sound rolled out, amplifying slowly. Earth heard Raven speak. She paid no attention to the words; she let the compelling power of them play with her sensual self. Her insides turned, a hot burning sensation flitted about the stone of her. Earth turned, folded in on herself, a shock of heat shot through her. It changed her surface, the very atmosphere surrounding her changed. The air was electric. Celia felt it. She sat under cedar trying hard to gauge what was happening to the air, the village and most especially to Stacey.

Ned arrived in an old blue Ford with a young white boy in tow. Stacey's mom was resting—she was semi-catatonic really. She hadn't left her room much since the funeral. She moved about the house to eat, wash and sleep mechanically, her motions frozen to her widowhood. Fearing for her, Stacey decided not to return to school.

Through the window she could see both men getting out of the car. Steve, intellectual Steve, was chatting easily with Ned. Stacey did not remember much about Ned except that he was her father's twin. It was so strange to see Ned coming up the path. Stacey realized they must have been identical twins. Physically they looked identical. It was like seeing her dad rise from the dead. She turned to let her mom know Ned was here. It would be unseemly for Ned to see her come out of her bedroom ungroomed. Momma scrambled to get dressed and comb her hair before telling Stacey there was someone at the door. A couple of minutes had passed since they had knocked. The house was not yet ready to let them in.

"Shall we knock again?" Steve asked.

"Better not. There is no man in there, you never know what state them women are in," Ned laughed at the impatience of the boy.

"Do you think they're home?"

"Where else would they be—they don't dance," he laughed some more. Steve settled down when he realized this guy was laughing at him. Stacey opened the door. Ned asked if Young Jim was in.

"He's behind you," Stacey answered flatly. Young Jim had seen his uncle's Ford drive up from Ella's house. Ella had told him to go home. Ned was single; so were Momma and Stacey. They wouldn't let him in without Jimmy there. Stacey knew why Jim had come up behind his uncle. She wondered at the complexity of their system of etiquette. It was unseemly for single men to visit single women in their homes unattended by a male relative unless he was moving in for good; yet should a young girl have a child without a man, no sanctions existed to make her account for her indiscretion. She imagined that was the business uncle Ned was here about. The change in their ways had not been thorough in her family. Ned's brother's widow was his responsibility. He had come to ask Momma just what that entailed.

Ned stepped aside to let Jim by. Raising his eyebrow he grabbed Steve by the arm, indicating that Jim must enter first. Ned's action gave Steve the feeling that different rules applied here in this house. He decided to do things whatever way Ned did them.

The three men sat in the living room jeehawing about next to nothing for most of the evening. Both Ned and Steve directed their conversation at Jim, which made Jim appear even more manly than usual. The women came in and out of the living room at will. Every now and then they teased all three of them. Tea was served with lavish amounts of bannock, oolichan grease and dried fish. It was a great party. At the end of the evening, Ned said he had something for his favourite son. Momma giggled. Her face took on a flirtatious look which she carefully directed at her son, but it was clearly intended for Ned. Stacey sighed relief. She felt a twinge of sadness that Momma came alive only in the context of a man's love, but she was glad that Ned was here to breathe new life into her.

Steve had been looking at Stacey all night waiting for a moment they could talk alone. She had carefully avoided giving him any opportunity whatsoever. Now they all stood at the doorstep admiring the gun for longer than was necessary. No one wanted the evening to end, although their motivations differed. Stacey wanted to see her mother happy; Jim missed his dad and Uncle Ned was a grand substitute. Ned offered Stacey's beau a ride home. Stacey shot her brother a look that was pure indignation. Ned picked it up. He was sorry but it was too late. He had made a mistake about the relationship between them. Mistake or not, he would have to take the young man home.

Ned came by each day, taking Jim in hand. Each day he got a little braver about giving Momma lusty looks. She got a little coyer, more modest in her response. Ned was different from her Jim. He was flamboyant and cheeky. His obvious devotion to Momma was almost shameless. Stacey could not imagine romance between her dad and mom but she could picture it with Ned. Often he would drive up with Steve. Stacey had to do something. She had to make a decision about this boy. To make matters worse, Carol prattled at her constantly about Steve. She began to sound like a salesman making a pitch on Steve's behalf. On the last day of school she headed in the direction of Carol's class. She could hear through the slightly open door the conversation between Carol and Steve.

"Did you tell her what I told you to tell her?"

"Yes, Steve."

"What did she say?"

"She didn't say anything."

"Come on, she must have said something!"

"Well, it wasn't about that."

"What was it about?"

"It was about Polly and her mom not being able to divorce her dad and some woman named German Judy she visits on the reserve. I didn't get it. Sometimes Stacey's weird. She says things that don't make sense to me," Carol half complained, slamming her locker shut.

Stacey turned to leave. What in the name of Sam Hill was Carol doing? She had said that to her in confidence. Her breath shortened, her mind rattled off a string of curses, names she had never before considered using on Carol. For some reason she felt cheap, like she had been traded for something, but what? The rage clouded her ability to reason it out. Damn it, why had Carol done that? Done what? She ceased to breathe altogether. The inside of her fought for some place of calm, some kind of momentarily relaxed place where she could take her mind to think this out.

The face of her dad came up. One of the few things he ever said about white people was when she told him she was going to go to university. "Remember, if they ever have to choose between each other and you, they will always choose themselves." Her mother had chided him, but he held firm to his conviction without arguing with her. That was it. Between her confidence and Steve's interests, Carol had chosen in favour of Steve, betraying her. She had never felt this Indian in all her life.

On the way home after school she wanted night to fold around her graceful and dark. She did not like the glare of the sun brightening the horror of betrayal by the one friend she had had at school. Graduation was so close she could taste it. Now she had to decide what to do about her friend. The bright light of day made the whole scenario seem almost lewd—obscene. She thought about the shallowness of the communication between them, the unknowns they lived with without curiosity. Not once had Carol asked about her family, and Stacey never felt she had to. But there was little that Stacey knew about Carol except what she knew about white people in general. Suddenly she felt lonely. She searched for a moment, a memory, that would give their relationship some substance and found none. Maybe we just can't like each other, she told herself, but it did not satisfy her need to figure the thing out.

Is it prejudice or a gulf of difference too deep to cross? Steve was self-absorbed. He had no idea of the gulf between them or the end of the road for her should their relationship fail. He did not know Shelly existed; nor did Carol know about her. He didn't know much about the complex difficulties that having a white boyfriend posed for her. What about her little brother's growing manly pride? Stacey couldn't help thinking he might feel betrayed if she went with someone from across the river. She didn't bother to stop at the arc of the bridge but hurried home to the half-light of her nearly windowless house. Ned was there with a chain-saw, cutting huge holes in the old house.

"What is going on?"

"Me and Jim are putting new windows in . . . big ones, brighten the place up a little."

"That isn't all," Stacey answered slyly. Ned smiled shyly and sat down to roll a smoke. She waited for his story to unfold. Ned had always loved her mom but Jim had won her hand; now that Jim was gone it was his pleasurable duty to take care of his brother's wife. He and Young Jim talked it over with Ella. Ella had gotten a "yes" from Momma.

"Congratulations, you old skunk." They all laughed.

The powerful presence of her father was not replaced by Ned but there was a certain peace in the house . . . definitely more laughter that he brought with him. He was effusive and kindly. He adored her mom. That was enough for Momma and Jim. Their story had taken the edge off her feelings of betrayal. Maybe what Carol had done had not been so different from what Ned, Jim and Ella had done.

Her mom heard her voice and came squealing through the door.

"There's a letter for you from that place—ubc."

Momma handed her the envelope. They all stood breathless while she opened it. Stacey closed her eyes before reading it aloud.

"You have been accepted into the Faculty of Education," she read, and burst into tears. "Daddy would have been so proud." They all fell silent. Ned touched her shoulder saying, "He sure would, honey." It was so hard to let go of him. She had let his name slip out unintentionally. She knew no one was supposed to utter the names of the newly dead in case they felt sorry for you and came back to remain forever lost and lonely, waiting for you to take them home. The moment was thick with her emotions. Her error only intensified their feelings for her.

"Ella says he's long gone, honey, don't worry about it. He left the day Ned came." It eased her conscience a little.

"I can't believe I did it." She looked up at all of them. There was a hint of apprehension on their faces. They would miss her. Vancouver was only forty miles away but it may as well have been on Mars for all the opportunity they would have to get there. No one wanted to ask when she had to leave.

"September third is registration."

"What's that?" her mom said.

"That's when I have to be there." She read further down the page and saw the words, "We aren't sure how your status as an Indian affects your enrolment in this particular faculty. Please telephone early so that the office of the registrar can sort it out with you."

German Judy, she would have to ask German Judy what it meant. She didn't bother reading the rest to her mom. Best not to spoil the moment by worrying her needlessly. She would ask Judy first, then let her mom know if there were any snags. She hated this feeling that there were always going to be additional snags for her because she was Indian. It made her feel so tired and so much older than she was. Every moment of joy was tangled and saddened by snags.

"Well, you better get those windows in before summer's up, Ned." They went back to their work. Stacey went straight to her room. Momma took a glance at her that said something like "If you want to talk I'm here," but she said not a word. The difficulty in talking to her mom had little to do with her mom or her. It was the chasm again, constructed of unknowns, that kept her from saying something to her mom.

How could she tell her what she did not herself understand? In her room day receded. Her thin little bed lay in perpetual dark. None of the bedrooms had windows, although Ned had plans for that. She wasn't sure she wanted a window in this little room. Stacey was convinced that the lack of light had hot-housed much of her thinking. Darkness had helped her to sort things out. She liked the total black at night when all the lights were out and there was only the inside of her mind to see.

Major decisions had been made there in the dark. She could see her whole life unfold ahead of her when she lay staring at the black in solitude. She watched her relationship with Carol unfold anew. The dark distanced the pain, until only the relationship remained. There had not been much between them, she admitted now. She had given very little; Carol had not offered much either. The difference was that Carol was operating within the context of herself and her culture. Stacey had been the false face. She felt that now. She had no idea what to do with it, but she felt it deep inside.

CHAPTER

8

It is going to be a long hot summer, Dominic had said. He hadn't been talking about the weather only. The epidemic was winding to a close but its impact was only now peaking. Ten days of blinding effort. Ten days of struggle. Ten days of continuous grief and defeat; then it should have been over. The controversy over the neglect of the Indian 'flu victims raged on in the paper long after the epidemic had died down. Their own death-count was terrible. Seventeen new-borns, one middle-aged man, six old men and the last of Ella's people had perished. Nora, Sadie and Ella were the only survivors in their family of the 'flu epidemic of 1919. Their brothers had all perished, one of them on the streets of Vancouver. Ella had recounted the tale one winter night long ago.

"Don't go to the city, child. Them people die on the streets and people just step over them and keep on walking." This was too terrifying for Ella to contemplate. "They just step right over you," she repeated, then wept. She wept not for the dead who lay on the street but because she was saddened by the astounding lack of humanity of the people who stepped over the dead without bothering to close their eyes or acknowledge the passing of a sacred spirit to another world. "He lay there, eyes open, until the truck that came to carry the dead away arrived." Her brothers but one died childless.

Two lineages were lost in the first 'flu epidemic and now Ella's sister Sadie joined the line of siblings in some place no one dared define. Quiet soft-spoken Sadie. Stacey thought about the old people and the characters they had become. Each seemed to assume a position in the community. Sadie was the *ta'ah* of all of the them. A grandmother who loved each child. She shed affection just by her presence. Children sought her out for loving affirmation. Stacey realized Sadie had never scolded or shot a disapproving look at any child in the village.

Ella sat looking out her window at the grandchildren her two sisters left behind, waiting her turn. The loss of old people in the village during those ten days cannot be measured. The controversy that raged in the paper focussed on the loss of babies. Stacey realized that white people couldn't conceive of the depth of loss their old people represented—their significance to the villagers escaped them, so they could not empathize with their passing.

Dominic's pathos was that he could not heal the community. He felt it was his responsibility to send this tiny animal life away. He had sent grizzlies, cougars, badgers and snakes away, but this little animal was unknown to him. He cudgelled himself each night for the secret, the key to the viral language of the illness. He induced dreamsleep, enduring ceremony after ceremony trying to locate the voice that would tell him what to say to drive the beast home. Finally, just before he died, he dragged himself out of his home and over to Momma's. Hong Kong was just too far away for him to hear the right words, he said, defeat and humiliation registering on his face. Tears flowing from his eyes, he picked himself up and headed home. There was no peaceful look on his face as he lay in his coffin. Defeat rested there to carry him away.

Dominic had been the caretaker of the law and philosophy of the village. As yet no other had come forward to take his place and now the village had no law-giver, no philosopher to consult. They were all like a rudderless ship wandering aimlessly in the fog. Sadie had been the keeper of their wild foods. She knew the medicines, the time of year to pick them and all of their uses. She too had died too without a replacement. Stacey wondered why no one had come forward to replace them sooner. Then she remembered Grampa Thomas. He had preceded Dominic. Grampa had been over one hundred years old when he died. Dominic was barely seventy. The village had thought they had plenty of time. Sadie was sixty—more than forty years younger than Grampa Thomas. Momma had been going out with her each season for two years now. It was not long enough. There must be a way. There must be some way to rescue this situation. Stacey flogged herself with the question.

Dreamsleep came fitful and nervous. She tossed and turned. She rolled this way and that, finally awakening in the black of night. The night was so black she wasn't sure she was awake. She touched herself. She could feel the touch. She was awake. The room's black was velvet. A song came. It seemed to come from far away, yet it filled the room. It murmured of things gone past. It memoried for her the assurance of a great awakening she should ready herself for. It soothed, finally it ended and she drifted into sleep. In sleep Nora's life returned.

Nora's husband succumbed to tuberculosis in 1936, the year Stacey had been born. The funeral had been simple, everyone said, and Nora had shed no tears. She let go her shovel-load of dirt and when everyone had had their turn she insisted on burying him herself. Stacey's mom had urged her to let the others help. Nora had refused. Her small children clung to their mother's side for the four hours it took to finish burying him. No one had moved.

In the hall on the night of Nora's husband's funeral, the mood had been sombre. Speaker gave his history, his clan story and then invited others to speak. His sisters came from Washington, where he had been born. They sang for their lost brother, wept speaking to the disease that took his life. Tuberculosis was peaking then. According to the prophesies the villagers had two more epidemics to endure. Others came forward, briefly recounting the honour of the deceased. He had been sensitive and artistic. He adored Nora. Even in her sleep Stacey could not conjure any image of an adoring husband for Nora. At the time Nora was "a little stiff," but not totally without humour.

Nora's mother was still alive then. She had not come to the funeral. Despite the fact that her English mother had married an Indian she had not wanted Nora to traverse the same route. If her mother's refusal to attend her son-in-law's funeral upset Nora she told no one. It must have bothered her, Stacey decided, rolling around memory for a while, reconsidering what Grampa Thomas had said about the difference between governing memory and the events which add to governance. It had confused her then but she felt that in this one riddle lay some truth she would need. Nora was forty-five when her husband died. As Stacey slept she realized Nora must have been in her thirties by the time she married. What kept her preoccupied between twenty and thirty-five? The answer escaped Stacey's dreams.

The man had barely been laid to rest when Momma saw Nora harness up her husband's old Clydesdales and head for the bush. The curtains of half a dozen homes moved slightly to watch Nora leave. Her two little girls, aged nine and ten, chugged behind their mom. Momma had hollered out to leave the little ones behind—Nora declined. No daughter of hers was ever going to be dependent on some man. Momma had gasped. What a thing to say in front of small children.

Shortly after she left, the village was busy. Because Momma had spoken to Nora so cheekily the neighbours ventured over to her house and the gossip began, heroizing Nora's courage. Dominic and Grampa Thomas came around and the conversation took the direction of a struggle for understanding. It was a rare moment. Grampa Thomas and Dominic came head to head; no one from the outside would have noticed that a debate was going on. Each couched their words carefully in a complex of courteous positing of their own thinking while exploring and validating each other's. For a woman to take up the role of father in these times seemed threatening. It was her choice, was what Grampa ended up with. They all worried about the girls not being mothered while their mother was busy fathering them.

"We used to have people like that before the blackrobes came," Grampa Thomas had ventured.

"Like what?" Momma had asked. He told them a story and Momma had repeated it to Stacey. It was a story of a warrior woman of long ago, long before the complex clan system even. Grampa called her "She," the nameless woman. Nameless not out of disrespect but for want of definition. To children she was mother and to the world she was warrior. Her duality inspired fear and reverence in her fellow villagers. Grampa Thomas began to sing. Momma knew he was searching for memory; singing helped him unleash the memory of his ancestors. At the end of the song Grampa Thomas decided that Nora and Rena were descended from this nameless woman with two spirits.

Not many of the villagers bought the story. It wasn't natural, many said, to which Grampa Thomas retorted, "We don't live in natural times so we have no way of knowing what is natural and what is not." Momma had accepted Grampa Thomas's story as truth. He was a thinker, the rest of them were not even curious enough to wonder much about anything. She and the others just lived out their lives gathering food, keeping busy until the end of their stay on earth.

Grampa was so busy thinking that often he would forget to eat. He was thin most of the time. Now that she was married and it was not unseemly for her to visit Grampa, Momma had taken it upon herself to make sure he ate at least once a day. While she cooked and cleaned for him Grampa kept up a steady stream of talk, mostly stories. Momma liked the stories. She repeated them to her children during the long winter nights in which she sat 'round the stove knitting thick socks for her small family and some of the old people too frail to do their own knitting. If Stacey's dad was not busy doing some sort of work or another he joined Momma, either spinning the wool on a whorl or doing the plain knitting. He never did learn to do any designs.

Nora would sometimes come by on these nights and help with the whorl. Like Stacey's dad, she could spin and knit but she knew no designs to beautify the work. Nora had teased Momma about her penchant for art. Stacey saw Nora again at her house laughing with Momma and realized that that was the only time she laughed. Momma had been comfortable in her flirtatious relationship with Old Nora.

She looked again at Nora's hands, large and strong, and at her body, lean and vigorous. She sat in the chair much the same way Stacey's father did, legs slightly apart, with her chest leaning into her conversation. When she was on a roll with some story or other she stood up and assumed the beauty and cadence of Speaker. Her eyes were large and shaped like Raven's, snappy and black, her skin dark but her hair auburn, almost red. She kept it sleek and tied back away from her handsome face. She was beautiful when she spoke. Her gestures were expressive, perfectly timed and graceful.

When Grampa Thomas died the old people congregated to choose another Speaker. It had taken them a long time. Dominic or Nora. They had argued that Nora was the better speaker of the two but they had never before chosen a woman as Speaker. Without Grampa Thomas to joggle the story of Speaker and "She" into place, Nora was not chosen. If their decision upset Nora she never let on. In the dark of the room Stacey felt a warm light pass over, sensuous and sweet. It touched the outside of her skin with silky softness; inside, her body purred velvet smooth. She heard a voice whisper, "Don't worry child, woman's day is coming."

CHAPTER

9

SHE AWOKE FEELING RESTED AND VIGOROUS, DETER-
mined to speak to Steve as soon as he rolled down the driveway.
She had a feeling he would come by today. She swept the place
out and cooked while her mother sewed new curtains from the
cloth Ned had bought her. Stacey wondered where he got all the
money to lavish gifts upon her mother, though she never asked.
Women ought not to interfere in a man's business, just as no man
would dare to tell a woman what to do with a piece of cloth once
it left his hands.

She had never heard any man in her village chide his wife the
way Mr. S. did his. Of course, Momma would not bring up her
Jim's or Ned's business by way of conversation either. Each kept
the other informed of their life but neither advised the other unless specifically asked. This simple dictum kept them from ever
quarrelling.

Momma looked up from the machine Ned had brought her.
She was going to marry him come spring, when her mourning

time would be over, she said. Stacey dried her hands after the last dish was washed and sat next to her mother. They looked at each other a little wickedly, then laughed.

"Life is so strange," Momma began, looking up for a moment, cocking her head to one side then returning to her sewing while she recounted the romance between her and Ned and his twin brother. It began in the early days of the Depression. Both boys visited Momma's house a lot. She winked at Stacey, giggling as she said, "I was beautiful then." Stacey laughed.

"You still are, Momma."

Ned was restless in those days. He talked of working in the city, gathering up some money then coming home. He wanted to live in the same kind of house white folks had. His wife would have beautiful pots and pans, matching dishes, curtains and lots of cloth for blankets. Although it excited Momma to hear him talk, she thought him arrogant. She was sure she never wanted to go to the city where people died in the street while others just stepped over you and kept going, so she opted for the quieter, less ambitious Jim. They both discussed a possible union with Momma with her old folks. After much discussion between all parties, Jim and Momma were married.

Jim had insisted they live separately with their parents until he had built her a home. The home he built was simple, spacious and fairly large. They anticipated many children. After three years and no children a decision had to be made.

"We still followed the old ways pretty much then," Momma sighed wistfully. "A wife could get divorced if there were no children." She had not wanted to divorce her Jim. Grampa Thomas told a story of twin brothers, one the father of children, the other the woman's husband. Stacey choked. She isn't going to tell me that Jim is not my father. Momma's monologue softened, became reverent, telling Stacey precisely what she did not want to hear. To prevent divorce and still have children she had spent time in the city with Ned—four times, in fact. It had hurt Jim but he had had to decide between no wife and no children or a wife and his twin brother's children.

Ned visited the children a few times during their growing years. His favourite had always been Young Jim. Stacey had thought it was because Jim was a boy; now she doubted that. Jim looked just like her mom. She felt her stomach turn. No wonder the priests think we are immoral. We are. She sat rooted to her chair, wanting to be someplace else but unable to move. In her mind, the simplicity, the austerity and the bedraggled poverty of the village took on ugly tones. Some stories aren't worth telling and this was one of them. She waited for her mother to finish and then some. She did not want to exhibit any outrage until she had had a chance to think this through. She wanted to weep— Dominic was gone, Old Nora had left earlier and Ella had never enjoyed Stacey's confidence. There was no one to talk to. She would have to deal with this one herself.

Her mother could sense her upset. After a few minutes she whispered, "Don't use their laws to judge me child, use your heart." Her momma could not know how numb her heart was at this moment.

"Does anyone in the village know?"

Her mother told her that the village had changed. Half the reserve at the time were staunch Catholics and were convinced their old ways were immoral. No one but Grampa Thomas and the twins knew. Not even Dominic. Stacey felt relieved. She blushed at her relief: getting caught was worse than the act itself, ran through her mind. She felt like Polly. A small knock at the door rescued her from thinking any further about the dilemma this story posed.

It was Steve. Her resolve to talk to him had left with the shock of Momma's tale. Her momma sat in the corner of the kitchen studiously hunched over her machine. She didn't look quite as lovely to Stacey as she had a short time ago. Grey hair sparkled between the strands of black. The ponytail she tied her hair in was loose and mischievous hairs escaped, making it look messy. Momma's slightly wild look had spelled passion earlier; now, in the face of her tale, she looked plain and messy.

Steve's manicured self contrasted sharply with the messiness of her mom. Steve remembered men never entered the house of single women without a man present, so he asked for Young Jim. This rule now looked absurd to Stacey—pretentious. Steve abiding by it annoyed her. The elaborate protection of female virtue meant so little now. She didn't let her heart reach her face lest Steve ask her what was wrong. She would either have to lie and say "nothing" or tell him it was none of his business.

"He's hunting. I'll come out." She closed the door, leaving wordlessly. She did not see her mother's voiceless tears. After she left, Momma went to her room to let the tears fall. She was on trial and Stacey, her beloved Stacey, was her judge. She wanted to weep, to have Stacey hold her, but she knew how coercive tears could be to a child. She could not burden her daughter with guilt on top of the tale of paternity that was no longer acceptable to anyone in the village. She whispered to Grampa Thomas and Old Nora in the dark before she finally slept.

Outside the heat was blinding. Despite the village's proximity to the West Coast, the earth had begun to crack and dry. Drought, so unusual in this part of the world, now scorched the village. The mint Momma had replanted in the yard had not grown much. Water was scarce: Old Ella told them not to water their mint gardens. Rain, the tears of woman-earth paining to give birth, was not forthcoming. The earth was barren. The rain that had barely wet the earth during a two-day sprinkle was all there was going to be. Everyone would just have to live with it. The children who played in the village centre seemed to be less lively than in summers when the rains relieved the heat and cooled the air. Stacey could see the little ones chopping at the dry dirt with spoons without any enthusiasm. The volume of their laughter was toned down by the oppressive heat.

"The gods must be angry," Steve quipped.

"The gods?" she asked, then caught herself. Just a figure of speech she said to herself at the same time that Steve said it aloud.

Old Ella's place had a huge cherry tree in the front. Stacey headed in that direction. The shade was not much cooler than the air but it subtracted direct sun-heat. Ella was in her rocking chair outside. Her grandchildren and Old Nora's scampered at her feet. The oldest brought her continuous rounds of tea laced with lemon. Stacey and Steve sat at Ella's feet.

"Say, how's Momma?" Ella asked by way of inviting Stacey to story her family's latest business into being. Stacey ignored the invitation and answered a simple, "all right." Both Steve and Ella gave her a quick look and old Ella laughed.

"He knows the answer to that question better than you now," she teased. Stacey wasn't going to get away with not telling her the family news, so she rolled back her disappointment and conjured their lives into being. She managed to lace Momma's curtain-sewing with enough humour to entertain Ella. The sewing was rooted in her romance with Ned.

"Oh, I bet Momma can hardly wait for spring," and they all laughed. Stacey tried hard to laugh with them but her burgeoning hypocrisy cut it off at the chest. She felt it rise sour in her throat. The sound of it was thin, almost tinny. She hardly recognized the laugh as her own. Her mom's romance seemed disgusting. Polly's face returned, innocently smiling up at her; she erased her. They laughed a little bit about how hard the mourning year is for women her mom's age, then from out of the blue Ella asked Steve to go to white town to buy her some lemons. She had been craving lemons all day. Her grandchildren didn't feel right in white town. Steve jumped to the mission. He had not asked her for the change to purchase them—he must have money of his own, Stacey thought.

"I'm old, Stacey, but I am no fool. What is wrong? You and Momma have a fight?"

"I can't tell you, *ta'ah*," she muttered.

"Then it must not be your story to tell," Ella answered. The arrow of Ella's understanding hit Stacey hard. "In which case you got no business being upset." She looked hard at Stacey. Her face took on a definite Nora quality, stern and loving in equal volume. She tried to figure out what Ella meant. She repeated the lines looking for the hook, the key to what would relieve her of this ugly feeling toward her mother.

"Child, child, child," Ella murmured. "There are only a few things that get kids this upset at your age—their mothers' morals, now or in the past. They tell me that there are big houses in the city, where white men live. They all own binoculars. At night they look through their binoculars into the big houses of others. We don't own any binoculars, child. We keep our minds and hearts in our own bedrooms. You live longer that way."

"I didn't ask for the story," she defended herself.

Ella hit her lightly with a stick she had been playing with. Stacey managed a weak grin.

"Don't play lawyer with me, child. I'm no judge." She laughed at Stacey's defensiveness again. This time Stacey managed a weak smile.

"I wish Grampa Thomas was still alive."

"Goodness," Ella retorted quickly, "while you're wishing, why don't you wish these people never came to mess up our lives." She laughed deliciously. "Must be some story." She winked lasciviously at Stacey. "Eh?" she asked, whacking Stacey lightly again. She retold the story of Snot Woman, a story full of risqué humour and passion. It started to read differently to Stacey. The loyalty of Snot Woman was tied to the ability of her silly husband to gratify her passion. Stacey figured out halfway through the story that Ella was giving her mother permission to satisfy her passions any time, in any way she chose. Polly was smiling at her again. This time Stacey did not push her out of the way.

She listened to the story without paying much attention to the words. The sound of Ella's voice, its inflection, the soft accent and the faces she wore in the telling seemed more important than the words. She let Polly's twinkling mischievous eyes roll around the story until she figured out why she was so obsessed with Polly. Polly and Momma were the same woman—good-hearted and passionate. In the white world her momma would have perished.

In her own world of choice and acceptance, Momma was safe. No wonder she never left her village much. Stacey got the notion that she had brought their world into Momma's house. She felt bad. Ella finished the story and looked at her briefly, her eyebrows up in flirtation; then she sat back and her eyes looked straight forward and blank with dismissal. Stacey got up to go home. Better settle this now before she had cut into her mother's heart too deeply.

The kitchen was empty. Stacey wandered over to the sewing machine. Fine water-marks of perfect little circles dotted the cloth. Stacey groaned. She knew her mother was in her room. There were strict codes of conduct about marching into each other's bedroom so she decided to wait for her to come out. She looked at the work her mother was doing. It looked simple. Soon she sat down and carefully hemmed the rest of the curtains. After she had finished one of them her mother came out.

The relief on her mother's face was palpable and Stacey smiled broadly at her. She was beautiful again, wild and sensuous. They never again spoke of Momma's story. It didn't matter anymore. Steve never came back to the house. Apparently he and Ella had spent hours chatting in her yard until sundown, then he left. Every now and then he returned to Ella's armed with lemons.

They would sit in her yard and chat and then he'd leave. Stacey had no idea what Ella had told him to discourage him from dreaming of her, but it solved Stacey's problem of having to shame him with rejection. The secret she and her mother shared brought them closer together somehow. In the weeks that followed Stacey spent as much time as she could with her.

She watched her mother's movements, listened to her voice and searched obsessively for the why of her. Funny she had not thought of studying to figure out her mom before. The confidence between them grew. Soon Momma was telling her about her own life. Stacey knew Momma couldn't read. One afternoon while the two of them bent over the sewing machine Momma told Stacey why. It was the second story Momma had ever told her about herself.

She had left for residential school just like the others. They were all scrubbed clean and deloused; even Momma, who had no lice, was deloused. It was such an indignity. These people had no idea how intimate a gesture touching the hair was. Complete strangers fiddled with her hair and cut off her braid. Momma cried. A lot. She cried day and night, nonstop for a week. Finally, the nuns sent her home. They complained to her parents that all she did was hold the back of her neck and weep. She was disruptive to the others.

"I was disruptive," Momma remembered with amusement. She treasured this little memory of herself disrupting the entire school simply by holding the back of her neck and weeping. Stacey told her about her "No" to the principal of her school and momma laughed proudly.

"Too much Raven," they both laughed.

10

THERE WAS A DIFFERENT FEELING IN THE AIR THIS morning. She glanced about her trying to figure out what it was. Ah, the smell of moisture. It must at least be cloudy. Maybe the drought is over she thought as she hurriedly donned her clothes. In the kitchen her mother was stirring mush and fixing bacon and bannock. Young Jim sat waiting for his meal. It used to annoy Stacey when Young Jim first began this practice but she had settled into it by now. Besides, the wood for cooking was always there and the meat drying out back was plentiful. Jim was neither lazy nor incompetent. He had acquired the unalterable Salish male practice of complimenting the cook, which somewhat softened his arrogant waiting to be served.

He behaved much like his dad had around the women in his house. He gave the impression his contentment in their company was complete. There was no place on earth he would rather sit patiently waiting for the women to stir the air with laughter, rage or tears, whatever they chose, while he enjoyed their presence.

Should they solicit conversation from him, his responses were always full and round and well-tempered with modest courtesy. Every now and then he queried his mom on the amount of meat she needed, the amount of dried fish, but mostly he carried out his manly duties with quiet self-confidence. He was thirteen today.

Young Jim would now be responsible for the food-gathering along with Ned. Until it was time for him to leave home it was his business to know what and who he was dealing with. Without outright asking her, he had tried to figure out the right hint to give Momma to get her to disclose whether or not there would be more children. He would have to engineer this conversation carefully so as not to give his mother the impression he was prying into her business or limiting her choices in any way.

"Spring will come before you know it," he purred. Momma knew something was up, but the mention of spring had not been a big enough hint. Young Jim had not acquired the subtlety of age, though he tried. He dodged asking her straight out, but failed to make his meaning clear. Momma mentioned how lonely she was now that her children were grown up and she was still so young.

"The laughter of a bunch of kids wouldn't hurt," Jim answered. She did not respond, and they all ate in silence. Nothing was amiss for him. The world was shaping up just as he had always dreamed it would. He was sorry about his father but glad about the way things were going despite his death.

Stacey got a lump in her throat while she considered her brother's future. He didn't seem to want to do anything but just exactly what he was already doing. Life's trials and dilemmas didn't seem to affect him one way or another. On the one hand, she wished she could be like him, and on the other, she wished he were a little more curious about life, more like her. While you're wishing. . . Ella had said, laughing at her.

Over coffee she told her family that come hell or high water she was going to visit Rena and German Judy today. Jim didn't respond but Momma mentioned that she had been putting it off for some time now.

"They're likely lonely for you," he mumbled in assent. "Must be or you wouldn't be so determined." His eyes twinkled with laughter. Both Momma and Stacey laughed. It was a little unusual to bear down and haul up your grit just for a visit. After tossing that about for a while Young Jim and Stacey left. Jim was glad of the trek to Judy's. Being in the company of women with whom he had no real business would give him a chance to think more about Momma and the future of their household.

Momma watched her children leave. Her years with Jim had been hard. Now she would have to consider children again. She wasn't sure she wanted to go through all the biting back her own pleasure with Ned because the children might overhear. Still, her world began to take on a brighter hue and she heard herself singing old nearly-forgotten songs while her sewing machine clicked out an ancient drum beat. She wasn't even sad about Stacey leaving, though that would change on the day she actually went.

As her children rounded the corner and headed up the hill Momma wondered what business Stacey had with Rena and German Judy. Confidences. Mothers dream of gaining the confidence of daughters, only to be disappointed by the confidences they hand out to strangers. She harrumphed at herself, remembering leaning on Nora rather than her own mom. Her mother must have stared out a similar window after her receding back and felt the same way. She never let on, though. Momma bit back her own heart and never again sought more than she got from Stacey. Just be happy she is a good woman, she told herself, and turned her attention to her sewing.

Neither Rena nor German Judy seemed surprised to have Stacey at their doorstep. If they were they hid it well. Stacey decided they weren't surprised because white women don't hide anything very well. Tea was up. The spacious kitchen was full of hanging roots. Some of them Stacey knew to be rare medicine. They would have to have gone up into the hills to collect them. She knew Nora did such things but somehow had not imagined that Rena would bother.

"When did you go collecting these?"

"Last week," Rena answered, pouring tea for her. "There wasn't much. Dry as dust up there."

"Looks like rain now though." German Judy offered the remark alongside sugar and milk. Stacey declined. She had no idea what tea tasted liked fully dressed with milk and sugar. The smell of the milk didn't encourage her to want to try it out. Anyway, the whole idea of yarding on some poor old cow's breasts to drink the contents of them later was repulsive. Judy alone drowned the taste of the tea in milk and sugar.

"Likely just teasing us," Rena almost complained.

Stacey didn't recognize all the plants. Some of the ones that hung there weren't ones her mother knew about. Rena's Aunt Sadie must have rounded out Rena's education because Stacey knew that Nora had told Momma everything she knew about the plant world around them. Her mind began forming new questions out of this paltry information. She gave up. She was always going to wonder the why of things. Seated in Rena's kitchen with tea in hand she reconciled herself to being nosey—another Nosey Nora. She laughed aloud at the thought.

Rena's brows went up full of curiosity. Too much Raven, Stacey recalled her mom saying. Now I've gotten myself in a tight spot. I'll have to tell her what I was thinking.

"How come Momma didn't go with you and your Aunt Sadie to pick medicine?"

"Attraction," German Judy answered, laughing. Rena blushed.

"Hush now, this babe is innocent."

"I'd still like to know. Come on now, I told you my question." Neither Rena nor German Judy were democrats, so this ploy to extract confidence simply because Stacey had confided in them was a wasted one.

"You're leaving soon, I hear."

"Yeah, some time early September will find me on a bus to Vancouver—that's if the legality of an Indian going to school in the Faculty of Education gets sorted out." What she came for was out on the table and Judy jumped into the conversation easily. She had taken an interest in Indian law since coming to live with Rena and assured Stacey that since 1951 this was not a problem unless she wanted to be a lawyer or to enfranchise out.

"And end up like those poor white waifs in the thirties?" Rena growled at Judy for even suggesting such a ridiculous thing.

"Or Polly . . . or her mother," Stacey added, indicating that that was not an option for her and she knew it.

"You're all right then," Judy answered, "but if you have any trouble call me at the office." Stacey nearly burst with laughter at the card Judy handed her. Judy looked a little hurt. Rena told her to relax: neither she nor Stacey had any idea how to give anyone a call. Judy sat still, not responding at first.

She wore almost the same look of disempowered silence that the principal and Steve had had, only the reason for it was different. Judy had felt disempowered by the powerlessness of her girlfriend and this young woman. Strange, Stacey thought.

Judy offered to show her one day next week. Stacey said sure.

"While you're at it, maybe you can give me some instructions about going to UBC."

"What do you want to know?" Judy asked, to which Stacey laughed again.

"She doesn't know enough to know the question," Rena said smiling.

Somehow the ignorance of Stacey had power in it. It was inexplicable but there were so many assumptions in the white world that had no meaning here. Stacey recalled for Judy that she had been at school for years wondering how kids got books out of the library before she finally figured out that she too had the right to borrow books. It took another half-year before she figured out how it was done. The gulf between them ceased to be a threat. The absence of knowledge of the other world was so vast that Judy could not conceive of its size. All three women sat in a complete state of unknowing. In an odd sort of way they were all equal in their lack of knowledge.

"Step by step," Rena urged, "tell her about UBC from the time she gets off the bus at the depot in downtown Vancouver. Tell her what she should do next."

"Well, she should find a place to live," and the women laughed again.

"Good idea," Stacey replied between giggles.

"Step by step," Rena said, trying to get her laughter under control.

"You're speaking to a pair of complete idiots," Stacey offered.

"I know that's not true," German Judy pouted. She wasn't sure if these two were laughing at themselves or at her. That they were laughing at the whole scenario escaped her.

By the end of the day Stacey did get the story of how to register, find a place to live and begin school. It continued to be hilarious; as German Judy got a handle on the depth and breadth of their ignorance she too began to find the whole thing amusing. Toward the end, she laughed on her own as she remembered for the two of them her first week at Rena's. Rena had gone into the hills to get more medicine. Judy had decided to put some good European order to Rena's house, throwing out all the roots hanging from the ceiling or drying on the counters. It had been so disastrous that Rena had just stood at the door with this crazy look of rage on her face, and then she had laughed.

In the middle of German Judy's story, Rena was hardly able to stand she was laughing so hard. Staggering from one end of the room to the other she imitated German Judy cleaning up Rena's house. "Look at diss dirt," she said in a perfect imitation of Judy's German accent, scraping the dirt off the counter with the imaginary root and tossing it into the garbage. Rena was leaning against the counter rocking with laughter. When her voice finally caught up to her she squealed out, "She even bought a garbage can and them bags to go with it." This was too much. Stacey had to leave the room. From the bathroom she could hear the hysterics of the women. She could hardly get her pants off in time she was laughing so hard.

Stacey threw water at her face. When she had calmed down she realized this was the first time the difference between white people and herself had seemed funny. Rena was such a character. They must really love each other, she thought, to have somehow climbed all the hills of complete misunderstanding. She came out still laughing softly and shaking her head. German Judy let go one last chuckle before attempting to pour them another round of tea.

"Where's your kids?" Stacey asked.

"They're over at Martha's. She thinks we're too crazy to mother them with the proper sense of discipline—too much Raven, she says."

"That's what Momma says about me," she answered, not really knowing what it meant. Rena's face got serious for a moment.

"Will you be coming back for the holidays?"

"Yeah, Momma plans to be married as soon as my year is up. I wouldn't miss that for the world. How many kids get to be at their Momma's wedding?" Both women found this amusing.

"Ned." Rena affirmed that she knew who Momma was marrying. "Momma will be happier with him. Jim was good, but too serious." Stacey had to agree, despite Rena's indiscretion.

It was somehow fitting for Rena to talk out of turn by commenting on Momma's choice, which was clearly not her business—she was definitely Old Nora's daughter. Old Nora used to ask Momma how her old grump was even when Jim was in the room. It always made him raise his eyebrows to be talked about while he was still in the room. Stacey decided to story this up and lace it a little with more laughter. They all jumped off on the picture of Old Nora being dreadfully rude to Jim and him just raising his eyebrows in perfect silence.

"Are you finished?" Stacey asked, nodding in the direction of the roots on the ceiling.

"One more day," Rena answered.

"Be nice to wander about the hills for a while," Stacey mentioned, careful not to ask to go along.

Rena took the hint and invited her to join them, provided her mom didn't mind. Stacey didn't pay much attention to the condition attached to it. Her mom had never forbidden her to do anything unless it was dangerous to herself. She agreed, though. They sat quiet for a moment. The visit was over; Stacey was just reliving its joy for a few moments before rising to leave.

Their house had a whole lot more window light peering through than hers did. It was a sunny kitchen despite the clouds outside that teased them with rain. The linoleum on the floor looked pretty new. Must have been done shortly before Nora's death. Her inability to stop taking inventory of the looks of the house made Stacey laugh.

"What?" Rena asked, already chuckling.

"I can't stop taking stock of the way everything looks—it's like an obsession. I do this grocery list of the differences between white town houses, buildings, and our own. I started doing it with your house, too."

"Why?" Rena asked, a hint of disapproval in her voice.

"Why what?"

"Why compare us to them?" Rena's voice lost the querying inflection when she said this, it came out more like some sort of an answer, forcing Stacey to seriously consider the first question. She felt uncomfortable; heat travelled up her leg to the pit of her stomach. Although she had never experienced shame before, she knew that the hot discomfort she felt arose from the humiliation of realizing she was being unfair to herself and her family. She stared down at the tea in her cup. She had to say something, but words in broken phrases whipped around so fast without stopping or falling into order that she just sat there dumb. Her words made so little sense now. Rena reached out to touch Stacey's hand. Stacey's eyes closed. Soft cooling tears escaped. Rena knew, she decided. She sat for a few minutes more, then rose to leave.

"Thanks for the tea," she mumbled. At the door she hesitated, stared at the knob for just a second, then turned to say, "and for the words." The first thank you was for German Judy's benefit, the last one was for Rena. No one in this village ever gave thanks for food to anyone except the originator of the food. Salmon was thanked for salmon, saskatoons for saskatoons, and so forth. Thanking the household for food was a strange European custom Stacey had picked up at the Snowden house, and she handed it to Judy because Judy was one of them. Judy appreciated the gesture. The last thank you was not full enough, however. Words from someone else which illuminate the misguided self require more than just a mumble. Both Stacey and Rena knew Stacey owed Rena.

The two women waved Stacey off at the porch as she disappeared into the evening air. Her brother, who had remained in the living room in total silence, was now close behind. Stacey could feel his presence. The intensity of the last few moments had not gone by him. She started thinking about white men again. She could not imagine one of them sitting demurely in the living room, patiently and silently waiting for an evening of women's talk to be over. None of the women had invited him to the table so he stayed in the living room. The conversation of women was not his concern; unless invited to participate, it was disrespectful to join in. "Oh quit," she told herself, taking a look around her.

Rena had been right. The clouds just teased them for a day or two, then the sun had dried them up before the rain came. Actually, it was Dominic who was right—it was a long hot summer. The lethargy of the village increased as it became obvious that there weren't going to be many berries to pick even in the hills and there were so pathetically few medicines growing anywhere. Momma's mint plants wilted and would have died but she picked them prematurely. Like a signal, others of the women who still cultivated mint harvested the pitiful stunted creatures in their front yards.

The usual hollering back and forth across the yards during mint harvest did not materialize. No one teased each other about the crop. Some of the women who were mixed bloods couldn't take too much sun. They came in and out of their houses in fits and starts, stood before their mint patches looking more like they were gazing at a coffin than a bit of garden.

Momma had taken to lighting a candle at the ill-used church in the village centre. Stacey wanted to ask why; instead she went with her one day. On the road Momma told her she was lighting a candle and saying prayers against any more illnesses. "Our medicine don't work all that well on their illnesses," she had rationalized. "Anyway, it couldn't hurt."

Stacey thought it might not be a bad idea since there wasn't any medicine. She agreed it couldn't hurt anyway so she followed behind her mom, made up what she thought resembled a prayer, and lit her candle. The priest was delighted by their attendance. Their section of the clan was known for their Christian recalcitrance. They had all been baptized, married and buried in the fold of Mother Church but none of them attended with any regularity.

He urged Momma to come to confession. She smiled at him, nodding, without ever intending to go. Stacey had rarely watched her mom interact with white people before. She never went to town with her anymore. Her cleaning days were over and they had been carried out while the owners of the homes were absent. Whatever family business existed in town was for the men, not her. And since Stacey had never seen her mom in church or at Rena and Judy's, she did not know how she would interact with the priest. Steve avoided speaking with her mom the same way Ned did. It was strange to watch Momma, who had licked her but once in her life, for lying, tell this priest a bold-faced lie and smile afterward. Stacey was about to wonder why she wouldn't go to confession when her mom mumbled, "Sick old man," as she went through the double doors.

" 'Sick old man'?" Stacey invited her to say more.

"Wants to hear about my business." Stacey knew what her mom meant by "business," and she wondered what this had to do with confession. Since she had not been confirmed a Catholic, Stacey knew little about their strange customs. Why her mom would accuse the priest of wanting to know her most intimate goings-on in her bedroom puzzled her. Patience was not one of Stacey's virtues; she was fast losing hers when Ned went speeding by in the Ford hollering "Fire" out the window.

Stacey and Momma ran in the direction they saw others were moving with buckets and blankets in hand. The young boys were already stationed by the river, passing bucket after bucket along the assembled line, while the women ran between the river and the house soaking their blankets and lashing angrily at the fire. Rena arrived shortly after Stacey. Martha stood in shock, watching the fire consume her house.

"Martha," Rena said, taking hold of Martha's shoulders, "go to my house. You don't need to watch this—it'll just hurt like hell." Martha left, water falling steadily down her gentle face, clutching her and Rena's little ones. Stacey thought she saw her age in that moment.

The fire raged with a will all its own. The dry summer had kindled the wood frame mercilessly. The burning contents roared angrily at the pathetic efforts of the villagers. Everyone but Ned was there; even the old snake showed up. He directed the older men with shovels to dig a fire guard. Martha's house was surrounded by grass and brush. It was one of the few which did not have a gravel and sand yard. Her home was close to Rena's and there was some danger of both houses being burnt if the guard could not be dug in time. The ground was hard from want of rain. The little boys ran for the three mattocks that existed in the village and the men bent their backs to the work in earnest. Rena hustled German Judy off to her house for the pick she owned, joining the men in digging, trying to protect her home.

Time seemed to stand still for Stacey. The first moment illustrated a photograph of group pathos. Every muscle strained in unison. All applied themselves to breaking up the dry sod, shovelling out the picked dirt, blanketing the roaring edges of the fire, then spitting little buckets at the crazy blaze. Beads of sweat popped out on each forehead simultaneously. The movement took on a rhythm . . . pick, pick, shovel, shovel, slap, slap, whoosh, whoosh . . . each separate sound made to the same beat.

Stacey rounded up the little children who stood next to her mesmerized by the inferno. The effort was heroic, but the fire raged like a mad serpent, consuming their efforts faster than they could swing their little blankets or throw their buckets. Even the hair on the heads of the villagers seemed to fly backward with the swiftness of their movements. Every face was contorted with the strain. Still, the fire did not abate. Five minutes later they stood in shock for a moment as the house caved in under the mountain of fire. At the moment of implosion they were all leaning on their shovels, picks and mattocks in a weird sort of reverie. That struggle lost, they bent their backs to the business of finishing the fire guard. It was almost finished when the blanketers and water-carriers joined in. To add to the pathos, they had finished the guard and were already leaning on their tools, quietly depressed about their failure to save Martha's house, when the fire-truck came screaming across the bridge.

They were still standing stock-still when Ned got out of his car. His mouth opened, then closed. His eyes wept. Momma took his arm and began a wailing song for the house of Martha. Rena took his other hand. Soon others joined them to sing this sad old song. Their bodies rocked together as each villager locked arms with another and they bent their bodies to the song. The firemen could get nothing from anyone until the song was done. They looked from one villager to another asking who was in charge. Eventually the old snake asked them why they wanted to know.

"Well, how did it start?"

"Shit," the old snake cursed, then spat, "what difference will that make?"

"Well we would like to ascertain what started the fire," the man said in an offended voice.

"Will it bring Martha's house back?" he asked, his voice rich with sarcasm.

"Well, no," the fireman began. The old snake started to sing again. This time he took hold of his wife's hand, singing good and loud. Momma later said it was because he was crazier sober than he was drunk. He had started singing again in order to calm himself enough to keep from throttling the stupid fireman. The firemen stood around helpless for a while then left. Martha and the kids joined the crowd. The song over, the snake took a collection for Martha. Then the men left, gathering in the hall to decide how and when they were going to build Martha a new home. She could stay with Rena and German Judy until it was finished.

Before he left Ned mentioned Momma had a lot of room, if that suited Martha better. Martha nodded gratefully. Stacey saw the nod, wondered whether Martha and Rena had gotten along with one another while they were growing up. "No use thinking about" came back at her as she went with Rena and German Judy to pick medicine. The world don't stop for anything, Rena had said when she asked Stacey if she was still coming. Stacey fell in behind, almost catatonic.

On the walk up the hill she let the fire scenes toss themselves about without really thinking about them. They were near the hilltop when Stacey realized she had not kept her end of the bargain. The promise to ask her mom's permission seemed so trivial in the wake of the fight against the fire. She laughed to herself.

"Well, share the joy, girl. We could all use a laugh about now."

"I didn't ask my mom about coming with you." Rena looked so enraged at this small indiscretion that Stacey took a short step away from her. Rena sighed heavily and laughed.

"You couldn't possibly know your momma is hell on wheels when she is mad. The only thing that would make her mad just now is an unchaperoned visit with her daughter." Things fell into place too fast. Stacey's mind was still whirling around the pathos of the fire, their pathetic efforts to beat back the blaze; now Rena had gone from rage to laughter that didn't seem connected to the fire, except that the moment of rage had blazed then extinguished itself of its own. Unchaperoned? What was she talking about? The show of relief by Martha at not having to stay with Rena looked even more confusing now. These were women. Then she remembered the old snake used to go by their house hollering "queers" at the women inside, and the light went on. Martha was ashamed of Rena. She must feel like the old snake had a point. What was his point? The implications were too complex and large for Stacey, the questions too multitudinous.

Rena waited patiently for her to figure it out. Simply, in Momma's mind this was an unchaperoned visit in the same way it would have been had two young men traipsed off up the hill with her. Stacey hadn't thought about it. These were two women. Then she laughed too. Yes, Momma would be hell on wheels, but

Stacey, not Rena, would likely be her target. She took to imitating her mother's rage to ease the tension. They all laughed until their sides hurt. They carried on for a time, then took to picking.

The roots were pitiful, all dry and shrivelled. "Better than nothing," Rena quipped, "but barely." After an hour or so Rena stopped, saying old Ella said that's enough.

Stacey looked about her and said, "Ella knows we're up here?" Rena just laughed.

"Ella manages these hills, girl. You don't pick anything without asking her how much and how long to pick." Rena's steady gaze seem to be studying her and figuring her out, storying up her character, the body of her knowledge and the journey ahead of her. Stacey had the strange feeling that Rena knew a lot about her already.

"What happened to your white boy?" Rena asked from her perch on a big round stone.

"I don't know, but I don't think I miss him much," she answered.

"Wasn't much to miss," they all laughed.

"Last he came by he was talking to Ella and never came back again."

"Well, old Ella could discourage God from nailing Mary." Stacey knew this was blasphemous but she couldn't resist laughing. The notion of Ella discouraging God from carrying out the immaculate conception was too funny to let go.

"Long as you don't miss him I guess it don't matter. Seems to me your momma had a hand in it too, though. She told Ella long time ago she didn't want you messing with any of the village boys till after your schooling was over." Rena let that sink in.

"She needn't have. I'm not interested in any of the village boys anyway."

"You want a white one?"

"No. I've got no interest in ending up like Shelly either."

"Child, your body must be dead asleep or you aren't Momma's girl." They all laughed. Stacey had not thought about it at all till Rena said that; then she remembered she was eighteen today. Her body must be sleeping.

"Maybe. . . ." Then she remembered her obsessive search for the why of things, " . . . maybe my body has joined my mind in the search for the why of things and just can't handle two things at the same time." It cracked Rena up. When she recovered she asked Stacey what sorts of things she wanted to know the why of. Stacey recounted the questions of the past three months. Rena stared with her mouth open.

"Honey, that's a very long grocery list. You think you can fit all the answers into your head once you find them?" Stacey laughed. It didn't matter.

"I didn't have any plans for the answers. It never seemed to matter. I just wanted to know, was all." They carried on till dusk, then headed down the hill before the sun got serious about going to sleep. Momma was waiting at Rena's house, her face afire with fury. If looks could kill she would have fried all three of them. Stacey hung behind so the other two could get by Momma as Momma moved toward her with slow deliberate steps. Stacey foolishly ordered up her defence as both of them went outside.

"They aren't single, Momma." A slap to the back of her head set her ears ringing.

"She's white and so she don't count," Momma snapped. Stacey thought that was mean. They made the trek home without speaking, the offensive slap straightening her walk. They sat in the kitchen stock-still. Ned and Jim left. The air was thick with Momma's rage. Ned gave Stacey a sympathetic grin as he hesitated for a moment at the door. Stacey got the feeling he really wanted to intervene but changed his mind. No sense trying to disrupt the order of things on top of all the anguish Stacey's mountain adventure had caused.

"The law is simple, Stacey, and this family lives within it. If your schooling persuades you otherwise, don't come back." And she left for bed. Stacey wanted to be little again. That remark, that single remark had changed her whole place in life. Were she younger her mother would have whipped her. But she was eighteen and had been threatened with ostracism. Never again would her mother ever talk to her about her conduct. No more patience. She would have to own her every action. She felt frail, vulnerable and transitory. Dispensible. She was dispensible. It felt too soon, too sudden. She was too wilful to trust her own conduct. For a time she quivered on the chair like a timid little rabbit the dogs had cornered; then she opted for bed. "No use thinking about," she heard herself repeating Old Nora's words as her body lost consciousness.

11

Sʜᴇ ᴀᴡᴏᴋᴇ ᴡɪᴛʜ Mᴏᴍᴍᴀ'ꜱ ᴡᴏʀᴅꜱ ʙᴜʀɴɪɴɢ ɪɴ ʜᴇʀ ears. She didn't want to think about them, to consider the hardness contained in them or their significance to her as a responsible adult. She wanted everything to roll back to the fire so she could make her decision anew. The story of Raven's folly burned alongside the words. Too much Raven. . . was this what Momma meant? She would get herself in trouble one day with her disregard for propriety and authority—law, Momma had called it. Law. Her understanding of this law confused her. What made it so important to be chaperoned if, as a wife, her momma could spend time with her husband's brother and not cause a stir of conscience inside herself? Where was the sense of morality?

Celia was already gone. She was already situated at her usual spot behind the band hall watching Raven. The song that was customarily suspended in the air surrounding Raven hadn't arrived. She waited patiently for it while strange things journeyed about chaotically in her small mind. Old scenes returned. The old ladies gathered the young people together at this same place each year. The atmosphere was busy—festive, but busy. Everyone seemed to be bent on cutting, gutting and staking fish to dry; *shtwhen*, they called it. Celia recognized the place in a vague sort of way. She knew it was on the road to Yale, but just where wasn't all that clear. Between the scenes of work, pictures of young couples rose up, the young girls smiling shyly and the boys grinning hopefully. The old ladies in the distance seemed to be watching for something. Then the picture changed; the old ladies gathered in some sort of house. They talked excitedly in their language about who belonged with whom. The focus seemed to be on what sort of children this or that dreaming pair would create. The old women were giving the girls away—again. Although the vision of the process of arranged marriage was not nearly as threatening as the vision of the tall ships, Celia cringed, then the images faded. She rose feeling a little empty.

Stacey never considered where Celia was when she was not next to her in bed. Instead she surveyed the room, feeling the lateness of the hour but not wishing to hurry to rise. She knew her clothes were just below where she stepped from the floor to the bed. She had not bothered to fold them carefully as was her usual habit before climbing into bed. She had shucked them as she crawled into the comfort of the blankets.

We have laws and this family obeys them, Momma had said. You can cheek all the white folks in the world, Stacey, but there are serious consequences for violation of our family law, is what Momma meant. Her only authority to govern was her sense of law, her familiarity and her agreement with it, and her ability to bring her children to the same path. She could not be challenged without the loss of family that that challenge represented. Choice as a child translated into duty as an adult. That was Momma's way of things. Her sense of things was unalterable. You don't break the law in the fashion Stacey had; there was a way to change it and

Stacey had been unmindful of the way. She groaned and rolled off the bed.

She had to fix what she broke. By altering Momma's image of her, she had broken Momma's faith. Stacey was not lawless, nor did she intend to be. She had considered the women as just women, not as any kind of prospective mates. Momma failed to see the difference. What did she mean by the white one does not count? How could Stacey know that the white one did not count? How could she not know? came back at her. It was not an answer she could accept. Polly came into view alongside Nora. Stacey was really losing it now. Polly and Old Nora did not make reasonable twins even in her wild imagination. Still they stuck there while Stacey tried to sort out yesterday's confusion.

Things were going too fast. Her thoughts roared through her like a storm of hurricane proportion. No, it wasn't just that. She was seeing everything too sharply, too clearly. When had this begun, this looking at every little thing with too much heart and too much clarity? With Polly's death. She cursed her and felt bad. Maybe it was bound to happen this way anyway. If not Polly, then someone, something else would have set it all in motion. She became aware that she was clattering the dishes too loudly. It reminded her of the one tantrum she had thrown as a young teenager. She was to do dishes, and Jimmy made no move to help. She chided him. He remained seated. Her hand moved to clip him. Her dad caught it.

"Only if you intend he should hit you back," was all he said. His voice was toneless, without warning, matter-of-fact. She looked to her mother for support. She was clearly on Dad's and Jimmy's side. Jimmy did not pay her the courtesy of being the least bit worried. He continued to sit in thoughtful silence without so much as looking at her. She wanted to beat him up she was so mad. There was a small twinge of doubt despite the five-year age difference between them. She had spun around full of indignation, dropping the dish she was holding. No one paid her any mind. She could conduct herself any way she wanted to for the moment. Momma was sure to tease the life out of her later, when some visiter came by.

It had been Old Nora who rolled through the door. The talk began normally enough but Momma eventually engineered it so she could share a laugh with Nora over Stacey's latest tantrum. Stacey laughed at herself now. Not quite, Momma, this one will likely be my last. Momma came out of her room when she heard Stacey laughing. She made some show of looking around to see who Stacey was laughing with. She gave Stacey a dubious look when she saw no one there. Stacey laughed again.

"I was throwing another tantrum and remembering the last one I threw." Momma smiled knowingly.

"That was a good one all right, lasted half the night. Thought sure we'd have no plates by breakfast." They both roared. They relived the moment by repeating the scenario, imitating all the players and laughing till their sides hurt. It was so simple to relieve Momma's anxiety. They were in the middle of this when a soft knock disturbed their joy.

Stacey moved in the direction of the door. Her jaw dropped when she saw Carol standing there. She was wet. It was raining. Half the neighbours were out there drinking in the rain. Momma and Stacey went out too, whoopeeing and wheeing around for a few moments before remembering why they had opened the door in the first place. Carol just stared at them. She had no umbrella and no coat. Her thin dress stuck to her skin. She must have been wandering around in the drizzle for some time to be this wet. The rain was sort of more like a heavy mist than a serious downpour. Stacey recovered enough to ask her in.

Carol had never been to this side of the river. Stacey waited for Carol to comment on there being no gardens, no manicured lawns in the village. She didn't. She looked about her with genuine curiosity, calculating without commenting on the difference between her own neighbourhood and this one. Stacey offered tea. Carol declined. Stacey bristled. White people were so incredibly rude. Stacey argued with herself: Carol couldn't possibly know her refusal was rude. Yes, she could. She could have found out before she came what the sense of courtesy was. How, research it? Stacey stifled a laugh. It didn't go by Carol.

"What's so funny?"

"You're sitting there soaking wet, hungry and refusing to eat and you don't find anything funny." Carol laughed too, then said that she was kind of hungry.

"Where have you been all night?"

"Wandering around . . . Mom and Dad are getting a divorce."

Divorce and Polly's face returned alongside Shelly's. Somehow Stacey did not want to imagine that Shelly's fate could happen to her helpless friend Carol. Carol would not survive poverty the way Shelly continued to survive it.

"I'm sorry to hear that," slipped out involuntarily. It sounded stupid. She could have kicked herself for saying it. Carol cried. Stacey wanted to tell her not to cry, won't do any good. The words she considered using volleyed between stupid and cold, so she opted to shut up and wait for Carol to make the next move. Momma came back in the house chattering happily, but the air had shifted. She looked quizzically from Stacey to Carol after recognizing the shift. She stopped mid-sentence and moved to where the girls were standing.

Momma was looking at Stacey for some direction. She had no idea how to react to white people's tears. Her hands moved in the direction of Carol's shoulder, changed their mind, moved toward it again, changed their mind again. She stood looking comically helpless. Stacey repeated what Carol had told her. Momma frowned. Surely she shouldn't still be caring what her parents do. She shrugged and got on with her own business.

Stacey had no idea what to do either. The only remotely intimate conversations she had had with a white woman were the ones she had had with German Judy, and they were tempered with Rena's intervention. Carol and she had never discussed anything that was not superficial. The epidemic of a short time ago had come and gone without Carol saying a word to her. Stacey had buried eleven close relatives without so much as a sympathy card from Carol. She was starting to burn with rage as she thought of it. Carol had a lot of nerve coming here looking for sympathy when she had been so uncaring during the days of the epidemic. What is it with these people? They can watch you die, then turn around and ask you to sympathize with the pettiest of troubles.

"So, what's your point, Carol?"

She wanted to take it back. She remembered old Dominic's words about the bitterness that follows unresolved anger: "We have a right to the anger of any given moment. What we are not entitled to do is hold onto it until it becomes bitter bile spilling out indiscriminately, so that the person receiving the anger ends up paying for the misdeeds of others." Stacey felt like she was making Carol stand in for the anger she harboured toward white people in general. It was unfair; besides, she knew what Carol's point was—shame. She was embarrassed to tears over the thought of her parents divorcing. What would everyone say? This everyone that held so much weight for these frail little women. So much weight it had driven Polly to suicide. She knew from talking with German Judy that everyone would talk. Her mom would likely have to move from the town. The town that Carol knew as home no longer belonged to her. Her people were going to ostracize her family. They didn't call it that, but that was the end product of their behaviour. Whispers would roll around Carol. Gossip, mean and cruel, would surround her if she didn't leave. Leaving meant she had never really had a home, a place where she belonged. Stacey stopped herself from getting too close to sympathizing. Carol after all had done nothing to alleviate her countrymen's ostracism. White people learn nothing from their stupid merry-go-round of pretentious and fake morality rooted in deception.

Stacey knew that was unfair. She didn't really know them well enough to say that. She didn't know Carol either. She told herself to watch her own arrogance—it was the mother of Raven's folly, this arrogance.

"Let's go see German Judy."

Carol lumbered after her, reluctant and bewildered, mumbling "German Judy" under her breath like it was a question. They arrived at Rena's house shortly after. Rena and Judy were sitting on the stoop enjoying the rain. They opened the door, preceding the girls inside. Neither of them, least of all Stacey, had any idea what they were doing there. This time Rena got the tea. She figured Stacey had brought this white girl over for Judy to fix. Something was obviously broken. Carol looked about nervously. She didn't like all the dead air space. She filled it by repeating her tale of woe. Stacey watched Rena bite her lip, crunching back a laugh. Stacey had to look away before she started laughing too. Judy scratched her head. They were the last people in the world that would ever sympathize with the disruption of marriage from the point of view Carol was obviously seeing it. The whole scene was so comical.

"Well, what is it makes you sad?" German Judy offered by way of getting some clarity on the subject at hand, hoping this might help Carol to come up with a response to guide Judy's ability to help her.

"Well, they are getting divorced," she repeated. She looked at Judy for help. Her tears stopped short. She seemed to be saying, "Shouldn't I be sad?" to Judy. Judy decided to ask more specific questions.

"Is your momma sad?" Carol thought for a moment, then admitted her momma delivered the information reasonably free of any emotion.

"No."

"Is your dad sad?"

"No."

"Then why are you sad?"

"I'm a Catholic," she whispered. Now it made sense to Judy. It was no clearer to Rena or Stacey, but Judy sat her down, put her arm around her and began to deal with the girl's trauma.

In the hour or so it took Judy to retrace the path of Carol's shame about her parents, assuring her Carol's virtue wouldn't be tarnished by the actions of her parents, Stacey learned a lot about Catholicism. She was astounded by the nature of the religion. No wonder her mother only went to church to light candles or utter prayers for better times. It was a sin to lust, a sin to divorce, a sin want to be loved if you were a woman. Carol's mom had dared to want to be loved and Carol was ashamed on her behalf.

This meant Stacey's mother had no virtue. She was sinful. Although Judy tried to talk her out of this position, Carol entrenched herself in her church. Without parents and without the dignity of community it was all she had to cling to. Carol vowed not to be like her mom, sinful and lustful. She would be virtuous. Stacey wanted to gag. Desire had not stolen upon her yet, but she was sure that when it did she would deal with it in good Indian style, free of anyone's moral bonds. Now she understood her mother's angry words about the priest wanting to know her "business." For years he had been trying to get her to come to church to confess her sin of lust. He was so sure she was guilty of it. With arrogant concern he had worried over the carriage of her soul to his heaven, as if that were the only destiny for the dead. Stacey hoped that Dominic, who believed the dead ended up in the same place, was wrong—our other world and heaven cannot possibly be the same place.

Stacey had to go outside. She was holding back a laugh and it wouldn't quit. Rena followed her out. Both began to laugh before Stacey told her what the joke was.

"Won't they all be surprised when they get to the other world and find out it is a wonderfully sinfully pleasant place!" Stacey and Rena laughed heartily at the thought of infinite numbers of shocked white spirits who kicked themselves for being such unfulfilled lustless fools on earth, only to find out it didn't matter much in the other world.

"Must be white folks got no real troubles to put so much store in such things," Rena said with a sigh. Stacey knew there were real troubles for white women who divorced, though she didn't bother to say this to Rena. She meant in comparison to the epidemic they had just battled and lost so many relatives to, this was all so small. There were forty babies at the beginning of the epidemic and only twenty-three by the end. The productive potential of the village among those babies was cut in half. Half the talent, half the genius, half the friends and relatives to hothouse them. It didn't even compare to Shelly's dilemma.

"Well, at least she didn't kill herself over it," Stacey said sighing, to which Rena laughed.

" That was an odd thing to say," she uttered after the laugh was spent. Stacey told her about Polly. Rena couldn't believe it. It was too crazy for her.

"Gawd, and you want to go out and live among them—learn from them? What could they possibly have to teach that was at all worth learning?" Stacey had not looked at UBC quite that way. It did seem strange that she thought they had anything worth learning to teach her in the face of this reality. Rena leaned against the post rolling herself a smoke.

"When did you start that?" Stacey asked.

"Long ago. I just don't do it very often." The light rain had gotten more serious during the hour of Carol and Judy's journey. Rena leaned up against the wall to light the smoke and pulled long and hard. Two pulls and she tossed it, turning to go inside. She hesitated for a minute.

"Is that your friend?"

Stacey had to think that one over. It was hard to say.

"Child, if you have to think about the answer, it's no." She went inside. Rena took command.

"Enough of this nonsense about sin, virtue, heaven and divorce." She rolled out some stories that got Carol and Judy laughing. She cooked them up a whopping breakfast which they ate heartily. Carol felt better but she still looked agitated. Rena sensed what was wrong.

"You haven't been home all night, have you?" Carol looked like she was about to cry again, when Rena held up her hand, stopping her. There would be no more crying in Rena's house. She had no solution to the girl's running away except to go back or stay away; crying would only fill the house with misery and no solution would surface because of it. Carol was an obedient girl; the hand stopped the tears. If she disobeyed, these people might not save her, and she clearly wanted someone to save her. Stacey wondered how she had managed to stick it out as her buddy for so long. I must be different when I am out there, she decided.

"You want to go home?" Rena asked.

"No," she said.

"Then don't," Rena answered.

"Where am I going to go?" Carol asked.

"Why, child, someplace different from home. It is all up to you now." Carol thought about this for a little while, finished her breakfast, then, sighing with deep resignation, decided to go home. Before she left she looked around the room.

"Where's your phone?" she asked innocently. It was too much for Rena. She let go the laugh she had been holding onto all morning. Carol's face inspired Judy and Stacey to join her.

"Honey, there isn't a phone here." Carol gave them all a defiant look and harrumphed off into the noon rain. Her stomping created little mud splashes. By the time she reached the edge of the village she was a muddy mess. Rena couldn't stop laughing about her. After the first outburst, Judy didn't think it was all that funny. Seeing Judy switch from laughter to offence on Carol's behalf reminded Stacey of what Momma had said about her whiteness. She began to see some truth in Momma's remark—she's white so she don't count.

CHAPTER

12

Stacey had had enough for one day. In fact, she had had enough intensity for the whole year. She craved the ordinary, some sort of light-hearted activity that would balance all of the crises she had barely survived and had not had time to figure out. She thought of her younger cousins, Martha's and Rena's kids, and decided to take them all into the hills. It was still raining lightly but it was warm. She chuckled at old Ella. Just three summers ago, Stacey and her cousins had been sitting around Ella's house, all of them underfoot and in the way. They complained of boredom. She told them to go climb the hills.

"It's raining," they whined.

"If you wait for sunshine to do something in this part of the world, you'll never get anything done," Ella said flatly. They had followed her advice, enjoying themselves immensely. The climb up amid the chatter and laughter of little kids would relieve Stacey of the burden of thinking through every little thing that had happened.

It had been a long time since she had paid much attention to the rest of her family—her cousins. They had been raised as a single unit when they were pre-school age. Until high school they returned to being a single unit every summer. As the girls withdrew from the school in white town they turned to the only thing that really mattered in the village: building families of their own, securing the food and clothes to care for them.

Several of the girls had joined in the fight against the 'flu alongside Stacey, her mom, Kate and the others. They were quieter than she remembered them. She turned over the distance between them in her mind, determined to try to close it. She stopped by Annie's house on the way home. Stella was in the kitchen canning salmonberries with her mom and her Aunt Kate. Stacey looked disappointed.

She had all but forgotten that Stella was now a mother. She had been down to Lummi the previous year, bringing a young man home with her. He was likely up in the hills cutting standing dry in preparation for winter. Stella's dad was out back with the younger boys building an addition to their house for the new couple.

"Saaay, stranger," Stella teased, delighted that Stacey had stopped by.

"Well now, what's your name again, child?" Kate joined her. They laughed, clearing a space for her at the table.

"Why the long face?" Stella asked full of concern as she threw her baby on her hip with one arm, pouring tea with the other free hand. There would be no walk in the hills with Stella. Oh well, Stacey thought, canning salmonberries could be just as much fun if enough of them pitched in. Stacey managed to get them all on a roll.

"You know me Auntie, I can't resist pouting about nothing." They laughed as though pouting were the darn cutest thing a woman could do. Kate picked up the thread of laughter, reweav-

ing old memories of Stacey's many pouts into a bright cloth of humour. The baby, already old enough to laugh, joined in as though
she wanted to be part of this bit of fun. It filled them all up with
joy. Stacey drank the tea politely, then started boiling water and
filling jars. In no time an assembly line of fruit preparation and
preservation took shape.

"Idiot's work," Annie quipped. They giggled.

"It's what I do best," Stacey offered. They all laughed at this
obvious lie. Stacey had not learned much about anything practical
in her life. She had always focussed on school; even during the
summer months she wasn't much help to her mother except to
hold this and that as her mom directed her to. She was not cut out
for idiot's work, they all agreed. She was a thinker, like Dominic
and Grampa Thomas. Everyone in the community indulged her
fancy for wandering off to think or joining the old people in their
endless debates over philosophy, white folks' ways and their own.
By the time old Dominic died he considered Stacey his equal. The
villagers knew this, though no one told Stacey. Because she was a
thinker no one expected her to know how to do anything. One
day she would be of great value to them. They were all excited
about her acceptance to this place UBC, where she would learn
how to teach their own babies.

"When do you leave for UBC, child?" Kate asked. The air
changed just slightly. They would miss her despite her negligence
about visiting. There was also this tiny feeling of trepidation. She
may not come back. She may just meet some white boy, like
Shelly had, get married, divorced and end up on skid row. Anything was possible. The city was a terrible place but it had a seductive unfair charm for young people. They worried about Stacey.

"September first," she answered dully. She did not want the
concern they felt, not today. She needed some ordinariness right
now. Kate sensed that. She shifted her own mood so the air would
change again. Annie picked up the cue.

"Well that's plenty far enough away," she said, closing the door to any moaning about Stacey's departure. The concern melted, drifted up and out of the room, relieving Stacey. She took hold of her cousin's little one, tossed her in the air, snuggling her neck as she came down. The baby laughed prettily.

"Just think, Stella, I'll finish on time to start this one off at school." They got excited over the prospect of Stacey teaching their little one. Right away they began planning the school.

"We could use that old hall. Never gets used but at night now anyway. Just sittin' there doing nothing all day long. Not right." Kate kicked it off.

"We could use the kitchen to serve hot lunches."

" The mothers could come and cook and visit their children at meal times," Stacey added, then said sadly, "They wouldn't have to go across the river ever again."

"Maybe she will finish," Stella said plaintively. This shifted the air again. Maybe it was the bane of adulthood, Stacey decided. Maybe there was just nothing you could do about the seriousness of their lives. Once you get to be an adult everything changes. You begin to see the real conditions you live and die under. No more happy illusions of bright sunny days. Her memories of hill-climbing and berry-picking took on new meaning. Instead of a joyous romp, the berry-picking became a serious matter of survival. Maybe there is nothing to be done about it.

"Of course she'll finish," Stacey said. The baby gurgled, then burped up her milk all over Stacey.

"There's gratitude for you," Stacey said proudly. The laughter rolled out again. Stella got a rag and wiped Stacey off.

Stacey looked at Stella. Time hung still, held in the air for a second by the two young women who searched their common thread of family that would bridge their current differences. Stella was a mother and Stacey still innocent. Stacey was full of foreign knowledge and the philosophical understanding of their own, while Stella was a genius with the tools of womanly survival. They both seemed to be looking at each other from opposing ramparts between which stood an invisible arc of family history binding them together. The baby straddled the arc. The arc, the strongest shape in nature, couched the little girl that they both held. Both women's eyes clouded. Both seemed to know that their childhood closeness would never return. Somehow this little girl was their singular binding agent. Stacey would shape her intellectual development. Stella would love her. Together they would create a child different from them both. It inspired fear and wonder at the same time.

Stella had gone to residential school while Stacey had gone to school across the river. In the beginning of their school years they had shared differences about their schools, but now each in some way was disjointed from the other. They had not discussed school for a long time. The two of them felt a disjointedness from the life of the village as well. Stacey had come to rely on the friendship of the adults and old people in the village because none of her peers lived there most of the time. Stella was at one with her peers but divorced from her elders and her parents. The child between them would suffer none of this. Still, the only elder still alive among them who had not been to residential school was Ella. The villagers who could wield the language in the fashion of Ella were few and far between.

What sort of school Stacey would create was taking shape in her mind when out of the blue both women put their arms around each other, holding fast for a while. Kate and Annie joined them. They laughed self-consciously after this.

"This is great. The four of us stand here in a clutch while the berries boil over," Kate commented, relieving the tension of embarrassment for them all. The depth of their emotions lightened and the rest of the day unfurled neat and ordinary after that. Jar after jar of berries got canned and sealed. Precious maple syrup was used to sweeten the fruit before it went into the jars. There were so few trees left out this way that gave syrup. The entire village had carefully cultivated them, re-seeding the trees after the fires of the previous century. Little care had gone to the trees since those days but still the women boiled the sap down into syrup. Kate mentioned that the trees looked ill this year. Next year like as not they would have to use sugar. Stacey looked at her aunts more studiously than she ever had before. Maybe the epidemics destroyed their ability to maintain the levels of effort it took to survive in the way they always had. One less person meant that much less effort could be spent tending trees who gave up sweetener only with great effort. There were no longer enough villagers who could spare the time to tend sickening trees. They would have to find the money to purchase sugar from the store in town.

"It's funny," Stacey said, "each year we seem to need money more and more as the source of our survival."

"Yeah, even the mystery of creation seems to want to slap us up the side of the head," Kate answered. Stacey could hear a thin trace of bitterness in Kate's voice. It surprised her. Stacey recalled Dominic saying, on another occasion, "We have an absolute right to the anger of any moment, but in our kindness, we must never let our spirit fill itself with bitterness after the anger is spent." Maybe there was no place for Kate to put the anger so she clung to it bitterly. Maybe not having a place altered the character fundamentally. Stacey started to see the old snake differently, then shoved him from her mind: "No use thinking about," she instructed herself.

"Do you think we live wrong?" Annie, asked after half a morning's near-silence. No one seemed surprised to hear her break her usual quiet.

"I don't think so. It's something else. Maybe we are being driven from our insulated little lives into the other world because they need something we have."

"What?"

"I don't know. It hasn't shown itself yet, but it will." They murmured agreement. Annie took a look around the kitchen smiling.

"Well, it sure ain't anything we own," she said, spreading out both hands to emphasize her point. They laughed.

Every stick of furniture in Annie's home was handmade just like the furniture in the rest of the houses. Her Tom was not as handy with a hammer as some of the men. The chairs were made of hewn logs, shaved only slightly so you still saw their tree origins, and the seats were made of woven rawhide. They were comfy but definitely not lovely. The table was constructed of the same shaved logs, heavy and awkward-looking. The cupboards were just shelves with thin strips of plywood lipping the fronts so nothing fell off. No pictures, no artwork whatever hung on the walls. There was an old harness hanging on the living-room wall, a leftover from Tom's dad's space-logging days. Next to it was an ancient drum belonging to Tom's grandad. It was painted with red ochre and devil's club burnt black. It hung next to the harness, faded into a comfortable antique. That was all.

No couches, easy chairs, magazine racks, china buffets or rocking chairs to invite leisure. Stacey looked at Kate again. She saw laughter and great strength on the woman's face. She could feel the devotion and the physical musculature of her aunt conjured by the endless work of family survival. There was none of the delicate femininity of Mrs. S., carefully constructed of avoidance of physical labour. None of the careful clinging to youthful skin through the use of a multitude of facial cleansers and creams. Yet, somehow, overworked as she was, she had a seductive womanliness that spelled beauty. Raw beauty, unpretentious beauty. A youthful vigour that was rooted in continuous physical labour.

Kate was smiling when Stacey finished looking around. Stacey had forgotten how sharp Kate's vision was. She could read the thoughts of people written on their faces. "Faces tell stories," she always said to her. "They shift and change almost imperceptibly with each change in thought. That's why the old people tell us to look at what they are saying."

"No rest for the wicked," Stella quipped, hauling the jars to the fruit cellar out back. Stacey undid the rings from the jars, hooked them through a string, tied them off and hung them up while Stella and Kate hauled the jars, and Annie entertained the baby. Annie, Kate, Stella and Stacey rotated the job of entertaining the baby. It was the fun part of the day so each made sure they all got their share of turns at it. Kate left a dozen or so jars on the table.

"Did your mom get out to pick?" she asked, knowing full well she hadn't. Stacey shook her head. Kate was already mumbling that there must be a bag around somewhere as she shuffled through a pile of oddments in a corner of the kitchen. Coming up at last with a strong old brown bag, she put the jars in it, then handed it to Stacey.

"Sorry, I don't have any spare syrup. The drought. . . " her voice trailed sadly. Stacey picked up the list ". . . The epidemic. . . the fire. . . natural catastrophe and just plain poverty disrupting our lives again." The air heaved. No one liked hearing it all strung together like that. They hugged each other again. It was a perfunctory sort of hug, lacking in intensity. Stacey lavished the sleeping baby with many kisses and hugs, then she left. The rain still wept only tiny tears. The wind was blowing slightly in the dark. It tossed the little drops in changing washes against Stacey's face. The rain would heal the parched earth. Ella had assured them all it would come and come it did. Too late for the mint, but just in time for the huckleberries. There would be fruit in the hills soon.

Momma was alone in the kitchen, hard at her sewing. She

looked as though she had not moved. Her hair was a bit of a tangle. Stacey wordlessly took a hair tie from the counter where a collection of them hung on little nails, ran her fingers through her mom's hair and retied it when the knots disappeared. Her mother didn't move or look up. Stacey had always been this way. This was the one intimate gesture she conceded to.

"Isn't that just like me?" her Mom said. "Can't even keep myself tidy," she said laughing with pleasure at Stacey's devotion.

"Salmonberries," Stacey announced holding up the bag.

"Ohh, where did you get them? Have I gone and missed the season again?" Stacey knew Momma always missed salmonberry season. She loved them, but she never bothered picking them. For some reason she missed the season year to year. She had come to rely on the dozen or so quarts that Kate always saved for her. Kate loved the fact that her older sister needed something from her. Stacey realized that that was what really annoyed her about Jimmy. He no longer needed her for anything. In their family structure older brothers and sisters are as important as parents when children are young. As much of the care is provided by sisters and brothers as by the parents. Loving younger sisters always indulge the elders with some need or other—usually a conjured one, that keeps the relationship of their childhood alive and balanced. It saddened Stacey that Jimmy didn't seem to need anything from her anymore. Kate often came to Momma for advice she did not need and vice versa. It doesn't hurt to consult anyone, Momma had taught Stacey. It makes people feel connected. Sometimes they surprise you with a better point of view.

"Where's Ned?" Momma stopped working. She let go a sigh.

"I should go talk to Kate," she said. Momma was having a hard time. Ned was about her house almost every day now. It was stressing Momma's resolve to live out her year of mourning. Jimmy's presence alone held her in check, but what about when Young Jim was in school? She looked at Stacey, wondering if the girl had any context for understanding her dilemma. She must have decided she didn't, because she said no more. Eventually she told Stacey they were out hunting. Next would be the sockeye run, then drying them. They would have to go to Yale for that. That would be harder. Out in the open air each day, refreshing sleep and watching Ned and Jim hard at work each day, the darkening musculature rippling about like that. She wasn't looking forward to it.

"You hurrying through this so you can be ready for drying?" Stacey asked, taking hold of the finished curtains and starting to cut the threads still hanging loose from them. Momma was magic with a piece of cloth. Everything her hands did with cloth transformed it into beautiful artwork, but she hated cutting the threads off. Stacey had always sat with Momma during the long winter nights of sewing—cutting threads, listening to her mom spin tales of yesterday. Sewing was normally winter work for Momma, but Ned had bought enormous amounts of cloth for curtains and Momma needed some excuse to get out of salmonberry picking so Kate could indulge her, so she had begun the project in early summer.

She nodded a yes. Stacey thought about drying fish. She had never been to Yale. She had been excused every season for some reason or other. This year she decided to go with them. She mentioned it to her mom. Her mom told her that she wouldn't like it. It was dangerous and she wasn't used to it. Besides, shouldn't she be reading some of her books and getting ready for this UBC place? Stacey would not be deterred. She could bring her books, read while the fish dried and there wasn't so much to do. With two of them the work would go faster, there would be less strain on her mom. Momma actually liked the idea of Stacey coming along. It was lonely by yourself. There were a lot of families there but it wasn't the same visiting strangers as working all day with your own. Besides, Stacey's presence might take her eyes off watching the men work. Momma wondered if men knew how gorgeous they look when they work.

"Well, we can probably pick oregon grapes and dry them at the same time if there are two of us." They plunged themselves into planning what they would need. Momma asked Stacey if they should build a lean-to when they got there. She knew the answer but it was her way to always ask her equals what they thought about every plan they were going to execute together. Stacey felt good about Momma treating her as an equal. She knew that Momma knew best. She had only asked the question to solicit a yes from her, but Stacey liked being asked anyway.

"What books will you bring?" Out of the blue it came, completely outside the context of the conversation. It caught Stacey off guard. She hadn't thought about it. She wondered what the question had to do with Momma. She had never been curious before about what Stacey read or didn't read. Momma never asked a question unless she had a stake in the answer. "Why do you ask?" would have been too blunt and rude, so she rolled it around in her mind for a while before answering. Momma assumed Stacey was thinking the answer out and just waited for the reply without nagging her.

"I thought I'd just bring entertainment reading," Stacey finally answered, unable to get a handle on the direction of her mom's question.

"Is that like them books with stories in them?" she asked.

"Yeah," she answered.

"You know, I always wanted to know some of their stories. I don't understand them people at all—how they live, what they do. Their stories must tell you something about them, eh?" Stacey thought her mom wanted her to read to her. She decided to haul along her collection of short stories that could be read to Momma at night while they relaxed by the fire. They would need a lamp of their own and plenty of kerosene. She would have to talk to Ned.

"I could read some to you," Stacey offered. Her mom got a look of consternation that faded quickly, then she let go a bored-sounding "Yeah."

Stacey saw the look, knew she had missed the mark somehow. What the heck was she driving at? Momma realized she would have to engineer the situation a little more carefully. Stacey was not as quick as she thought she was. She wanted to be Stacey's first student. Oh well, once they were there and Stacey had the books in her hands, she could ask her how she knows what they say. It would all work out. It would be the only chance Momma would get to learn to read. She could surprise Ned and Jimmy. They'd be so proud of her. Next winter instead of sewing so much, she could just nonchalantly pull out one of Stacey's old books and start reading to them. Tears formed behind her eyes. She cursed her silly old heart. It didn't help; they fell. She tried to shift the cloth around so they wouldn't drop on it and give her away. One of the little rascals landed on her cloth. She ignored it. The escaped tear stopped the rest, thank goodness. Stacey didn't notice her mom's tears but she did notice the intensity of the air sharpen.

They stopped around midnight. Momma chided Ned for wanting so many windows and so big. She doubted the smarts of glass walls. What if there was an earthquake? Isn't there some sort of crack in the earth near here?

"What's even more ridiculous is us sewing for hours on end to cover the glass." They both laughed. Momma's grumbling wasn't serious. It delighted her to think that some man would bust his butt to build her a house like those women in white town have, with big bay windows and beautiful curtains. Ned had plans for her house. He was going to haul topsoil. "Whatever the hell that is," Momma had grumbled. "Then he tells me I'm to spread it all over the yard so I can grow things there. Means to make more work for me then I need." Stacey just laughed.

"I love you, Momma."

"What brought that on?" her mom asked.

"You're funny, is all."

"Funny?"

Stacey teased her about how proud she was that Ned liked her so well. It put her mom on a different kind of roll, naughty talk full of risqué banter was about to finish the evening off, but somehow in the middle of her mom's antics, visions of Polly, Carol and their mothers intruded on Stacey's joy. She couldn't imagine Mrs. S. and Carol sharing this kind of joy. Not after the discussion she had heard between German Judy and Carol anyway. What was it Steve had said, it wasn't just the getting caught, Polly wasn't well loved at home?

Images of the old snake down the road trotted about in her mind. Somehow the old snake's behaviour did not fit the neat and tidy condition of white town. There was something really wrong with that old snake. He was half-drunk, unclean most of the time. No self-respect. She remembered her mom telling her about when he returned to the village after the war. He hadn't participated in the war, but he had left with the others to sign up. He was rejected by the army for some reason or other. He ended up working on the railroad for a long time—six years. Then when the white boys returned the railroad bosses had let him go. His union had not protected him. White boys come first, they had all but told him. Acid rage filled him with hate.

Maybe that was it. Maybe some folks are just eaten alive by the hate and humiliation they sometimes butt up against because they have no place to empty it out. The old snake made his wife pay dearly for this hate. What was amazing was how much she tolerated it. She was different from the villagers, Stacey knew that. She had come from elsewhere. Why any woman agreed to leave the safety of her family to marry out was beyond Stacey. She did not understand why her cousin had consented to that; no one else did.

It made Stacey wonder where Young Jim would end up. The Yale gathering each year put men in touch with women and eventually the young men would leave and a new bunch of men would come to the village. The women of the village had a way of making these men aware that they were cherished sisters and daughters. They were kind to these men when they came, but the first week or two they teased them a great deal about the value of their wives and how fortunate they were to come to this village and become a part of the good people here. Only the old snake never left.

After the old snake returned from working with white town rail-workers he came back full of crazy notions about his wife's place. "I am the head of my household," he bragged to everyone in the village. He even thumped his chest. He said crude things to young boys about making women mind. People thought he was crazy, but Stacey wondered how long they would continue to think this way. A gloomy feeling that life was changing in the village loomed about.

Just last winter, the family's women had had to congregate because one of the men had beaten his wife. The man responsible was warned about the penalty for abusing their relative. Shortly after, the couple moved. The family had tried to persuade her of the folly of going with him, but to no avail. The girl was mostly illiterate—another crippled two-tongued product of residential school, so she never wrote to anyone about what was happening with her. Rumours abounded about the fate of young Gertie, but nothing concrete or tangible was known about her. Stacey had not thought about Gertie for some time. She was the daughter of Momma's cousin, not a close relative. Maybe her apathy about Gertie's fate had something to do with it all. She killed this notion quickly—"No use thinking about" echoed violently in her mind. She felt like telling Nora to shut up out loud but resisted.

The old snake had brought a piece of white town with him to the village. Stacey knew Shelly had been abused and discarded by a white man. It's how they are, she thought. They don't really like us. It was almost to be expected, but this man had been one of their own at one time. Now the old snake was just like them and he had influenced this young man to emulate him. Stacey decided he was dangerous. She couldn't know then that some of the families were already changed. She couldn't know that her own clan was the last of the families to cling to their ancient sense of family and that this was going to break down steadily as white town invaded their village. She had no idea how innocent she was. The departure of two of her women relatives was the beginning of a huge cultural shift that would wreak havoc in her village much later.

Tonight she just had this unidentifiable foreboding about the vague link between Polly, Shelly, Carol and the young woman who left the village to follow her husband. She needed to understand. She stared at her mom. Her mom couldn't possibly answer her question; she knew nothing about those people. Stacey figured her desire to know was somehow connected to the foreboding sensation she was caught in. The young women were changing; so were the men. What was the attraction of white town? Why did it so quickly transform our own into miserable wretches?

"One of my classmates killed herself," she announced.

"She what?" Momma's body convulsed. Stacey told her the story of Polly, as much as she knew of it. She talked about how she had spent the past two months turning it over in her mind, trying to figure out how it happened. Momma wept. She wept for this child she had never seen. It inspired tears in Stacey. Momma shook her head in helpless consternation. This was beyond her knowledge, to kill yourself. It was so unthinkable.

"Grampa Thomas warned us. If we eat like them we'll go crazy like them," Momma said. "It must be how they live." Somehow Stacey doubted this. How could food make them crazy? Grampa

Thomas was wise in their ways but Stacey doubted that he could know so much about white folks that this pronouncement would make sense. She watched herself eating dinner on Friday with the Snowdens. The food was definitely different. Instead of bannock, gorgeously tasting fresh white bread was set out. Vegetables were all delightfully cooked until they were so soft they fairly melted in the mouth. In place of the maddening fish, fish, fish were potatoes and meat, pork usually, roasted or fried. At school they were taught that meat was essential to a healthy diet. Milk too. Few people in the village could afford pork or milk or anything that was sold in the stores of white town.

Her own village ate berries, roots and herbs, and drank whatever wild tea was available. What meat they ate was hunted but only if the fish-run had not been great. No eggs, no cheese, nothing sweeter than berries was ever consumed. The Snowdens drank wine at every meal, Mr. and Mrs. Snowden that is, while the kids drank liberally of some concoction they named "Kool-Aid." Stacey had tried the Kool-Aid but it sickened her slightly so she always excused herself, asking for water instead when it came around. Stacey knew some of the villagers had wine fermenting in their cellars but not very many ever got to drink it on any kind of a regular basis. No one bothered to buy Kool-Aid for their kids. Her own family didn't like wine. "Not our way," Dominic had said. The few who did make wine generally drank it until it was gone. Sometimes it made them act a little crazy but generally the village was dry most of the year.

It didn't seem possible to Stacey that the difference in their eating habits could make you crazy. It must be something else. She tried to tell her mom how different white people were inside themselves. The littlest things were governed by the most complex rules and regulations. Someone was always in charge in their world. There was someone constantly watching over your shoulder policing your every move. It seemed that you were always in danger of being punished every moment. She could tell that Momma didn't really believe her.

"How can you live that way?" she scoffed.

Stacey recounted her first day of school to her mom. The teacher made all the kids line up two by two. Carol and Stacey were the last two in line. They marched the kids around the school showing them where they were to play, where the bathrooms were and where they were to eat. Stacey hadn't known that violation of any of the places in which a certain thing was done was discouraged by physical punishment. The teacher told them they would get the strap for violating any rules. Stacey thought it odd that violating rules resulted in a gift but she said nothing at the time.

Later that day she went into the library to search for a book. She was eating her bannock. The librarian grabbed her by the ear and started charging down the hall with her in tow. It hurt. Stacey pinched the librarian's hand to make her let go after repeated requests failed to produce results. The librarian squealed, then grabbed both her hands and led her to the principal's office. Inside he bellowed at her, then told her to hold out her hand. She did. He gave her the strap. The strap, she learned, was a leather belt that he hit you with. She was in shock for the rest of the day. She had not been willing to hold her hand out again. It took her a couple of weeks to figure out that these rules were sacred to these people.

"Rules and bizarre forms of punishment, not their God, govern them," she ended softly. Her mother stared at her. She had no idea how horrible school had been for Stacey. The force of Stacey's words tormented her. She had turned her only daughter over to these people who beat her for not obeying rules which had no meaning.

"What difference does it make which bathroom you used or where you ate your bannock?" Disbelief twined itself with dismay forming a yarn of confused horror inside her. Stacey would not tell such a horrific lie. It must be true, but why? She started to weep. She felt enormous guilt folding in on her. What had she done to her child? This tiny child, so perfect and sweet had had to endure twelve years of torment by these people, for crimes so miniscule they were without validity. Stacey watched her mother's face run through a number of disturbing emotions. She was sorry she had told her mother this story of her first weeks at school.

"It really wasn't all that bad. I learned to obey the rules, even though I'm still not sure I understand them. It wasn't all that bad," she stammered gently, trying to ease her Momma's tension.

Momma got furious. She scolded Stacey soundly. "Don't make small of this. You'll likely become like them when you start your own school." She rested for a while, then began again. " We have family in those places. We have to get them out of there. Will they do any of these things to you at this new place, UBC?"

Stacey smiled at her mom's innocence. "No," she said laughing, "university is for adults. By the time you get there you are well-trained in obeying the rules. They assume everyone agrees with them. Anyone who doesn't will try hard to live with them anyway." Her mom looked relieved.

"No wonder these people kill themselves," she said. "They don't value their own children. No small wonder they don't like us if they don't like their own." This last remark took Stacey aback. She had no idea her mother ever wondered about how these people thought about us. She said it like this was the answer to a question that had plagued her for a long time. Momma was strange. She never articulated a question beforehand to anyone, never threw out what she thought about; now out of the blue she tossed an answer into the ring that hinted that she had always been thinking about such things as plagued Stacey. At the same time, Stacey felt content that she wasn't the only one that searched out the why of things. She half laughed as she realized that she too was pretty secretive about the questions which dogged her. This was the first time she ever tossed some subject into the ring of her mother's thinking. Until now, she had entrusted her thoughts only to the old people and herself. She was reminded again of the kitchen conversation at the Snowdens.

Carol was constantly throwing out questions at her parents—not the same sort of questions Stacey and her mother had just exchanged, but nonetheless they seemed to find intellectual discussion free and easy. Current events like the 'flu, the controversy over communism in Russia, the segregation laws of South Africa were tossed about and conclusions arrived at. Until now Stacey had supposed that white families held these nightly consultations because they had no wise people in their families to consult, and so they had to muddle through questions collectively to try to figure things out. Confusion began settling in again as Stacey wondered why people in her household didn't have the same kinds of discussions as the Snowdens.

The differences between the villagers and white folks stretched. The gulf widened. Stacey looked hard at the gulf. She wondered about her obsession with going to their university and her family's faith in the sanity of her obsession. "How else are we to learn how we are to live with them?" Dominic had said. Both Old Nora and Ella had agreed. Was that it? she wondered. Is the whole point of her going to UBC to learn how to live with them? She was tired. Looking is so hard.

CHAPTER

13

SLEEP HADN'T RESTED STACEY WHEN SHE COULD HEAR Momma's voice, as though from a long way off, telling her to get up. She groaned. The urgency in Momma's voice reached her ears. She stirred and tried hard to wake up. Momma repeated herself. Very unusual. Something must have gone terribly wrong. She sat up and Momma told her again to get up. She jumped up, dressing quickly.

"The old snake has been shot."

"What?"

Momma said it again. "Who shot him?" Stacey asked.

"What difference does it make?" her mom answered. The implications of someone shooting someone hit Stacey. The police would be all over the reserve by morning. They would have to report it. Someone would have to be punished. Someone would have to go to jail, likely for a long time.

"Is he dead?"

"Not yet," her mom answered. She handed Stacey a sheet, telling her to start ripping it while Momma got in Ned's car. Young Jim was already up hauling the big canner to the car. Mom pulled cattails and bitter root from the ceiling. Stacey stared at her mom as she realized she meant to save the old snake. She hoped it was not for his sake but for the sake of the person who did the shooting. It must have been his wife. She must have gotten sick and tired of his violence.

"Good grief," Stacey mumbled as she stumbled into the car tearing the sheet as she crunched into the seat at the back. They sped down toward the end of the village under the cover of night.

"So far only the chief knows," Ned said. Stacey had not seen or thought about him all summer. There wasn't much to do as chief in this village. During the 'flu epidemic the chief had not been called upon by the local newspapers for any comment, unlike the chiefs in North Vancouver. He was invisible until some crisis which involved the government came up. Mostly the families took care of their own, but this would bring his authority into play. He alone had the authority to deal with the law and those outside who enforced the law on them. Neither the Indian agent nor the police could come onto the reserve unless specifically called by him. Mostly, he never called them. He might have to if they could not save the miserable snake. Stacey wanted to say something about the complete absence of justice in his poor wife's life, but she sat quietly ripping the sheet instead.

The chief was at the house. He hurried the women in. Those who were Christian mumbled prayers for the old snake as they entered. Others took up stations of function, boiling water or preparing poultices for Momma. His wife sat at her table, the gun still in her hand. The chief shrugged. So far he had been unable to persuade her to part with it. The old snake was on a cot next to the stove. Likely the chief had put him there, because there was a huge pool of blood next to the stove.

"Clean that up, Jim," Momma ordered. Ned and Jim set to

work cleaning up the blood. It had stained the floor. They gave up, told Momma and Stacey that they would have to replace the floor boards, and left. Kate arrived shortly after Momma and Stacey.

"How alive is he, Momma?" she asked.

"Not very." Stacey was suddenly aware that they were whispering.

"Why are we whispering?" she asked. The two women couldn't help but laugh.

"It ain't like there's anyone here who cares is there?" Kate blurted out. Both Stacey and her aunt chuckled again.

"Shame on you both," Momma scolded, holding her own laugh back.

The chief finally decided that the job of getting the snake's wife to relinquish the weapon was bigger than he was, so he went to get Speaker. Stacey wondered where she was from, this nameless woman without family, without beginning or end. Who would they contact if the snake died?

"Where is she from?" she said aloud.

Kate looked in the direction of the woman with the gun. Memory foggy and old tried to surface. She had known once but couldn't call it back. She stared at the features of the woman. Her cheekbones were higher, more prominent than theirs; her face had none of the fleshiness of their own people. Her chin had once been neatly carved. Her face had had a beautiful chiselled look before the snake had rearranged it. Now with her nose broken, her jaw out of place, and her chin looking deranged, it was hard to tell her national origins at all. Momma took one glance at her.

"Manitoba Saulteaux," she said.

"That's right." Kate remembered now. When the woman came she had thought there were only Cree east of the Rockies. It had surprised her to hear there were all kinds of different Indians back there. She had visited her a couple of times before she learned that each visit brought the old snake's wrath down on his wife. He was convinced that Kate went there to poison his wife's mind, turning her against him. "Crazy old fool, now look at you," Kate mumbled. "Near-dead and looking twice as ugly."

"She missed both heart and lungs," Momma said aloud. There was a noise from behind. Stacey turned. The woman was on her feet, aiming her weapon again. All three of the women stared at her, paralysed. She was going to try again. She must have heard them say she missed. Momma shifted. She stood directly in front of the cobalt blue gun. Stacey's blood pounded. Kate grabbed Momma and tried to pull her back. Momma didn't move. Stacey felt hysteria coming on. Her fear swam wildly around inside. Kate tugged harder. Still, Momma didn't budge. Sick fear froze Stacey. She waited, heard the woman instruct Momma to move. The woman raised her gun. She got ready to shoot Momma. "No." Stacey tried to shout but her mouth froze and the word died in her throat.

"Don't be ridiculous," Momma commanded. "The old snake's not worth hanging for." Stacey didn't hear anything after that. The woman's hand shook. Her eyes got this crazy wild look in them. She was torn. She had no interest in killing Momma, but she was determined to empty the blood of the snake. She wanted to watch it spill all over, steadily robbing him of his life the way he had robbed her of hers. She did not want to add another failure to the list of failures he had constantly punished her for. One success was all she needed. In the moments she spent thinking this through Ned had pulled up. The door opened noisily. She turned, Momma grabbed the barrel of her gun, shifting it skyward. The gun went off and Stacey lost consciousness.

She awoke screaming. Kate held her. Her arms were out of control. Her whole body convulsed. Kate couldn't hold her still. Ned grabbed her and rocked her, singing some old Indian song, and she faded again. She awoke a second time. This time she was under some control. Ned smiled.

"Momma's O.K.," and Stacey wept long deep sobs of relief.

"Good grief, child, you'll make yourself sick," Kate scolded.

After her crying stopped Ned told her what had happened. Jim had entered first. He saw the weapon aimed at Momma and leapt for it. Momma leapt for the barrel. The woman spun around to shoot Jim but Momma grabbed the barrel just in time to secure a miss. The woman shot the light out, and maybe the darkness brought her to her senses because she screamed "No!" as she dropped to her knees. By the light of kerosene lamps and some candles Momma and Kate rescued the snake.

It had all been so fast. The chief was there with Ella. They spoke in low tones in the corner. A decision had to be made here. No one wanted to turn this woman in to the authorities, but she clearly couldn't stay here. It wasn't entirely her fault either. The old snake had brought it on himself. It was all so new. Stacey could feel the tension of indecision. She had never before experienced confusion among the decision-makers of her village.

Everyone had the feeling that there was more to be considered than who shot whom. While the woman was not one of them, the children were. An unanswered question seemed to hang in the air. Momma fell silent, her face taking on a deep sadness. She retreated to the corner of the old shack and stared out at the villagers. Conversation came slowly. Long pauses dotted the tension between words. Each speaker sighed deeply after speaking. Kate wordlessly, mechanically blotted the flow of blood from the chest of the snake, casting a glance at Momma every now and then. Even old Ella seemed puzzled—maybe even fearful. It was not a night anyone wanted to remember.

Kate quit tending to the snake long enough to put the water on to boil for tea. She rummaged around the various little piles of kitchen things.

"The ol' snake didn't waste much time building cupboard

space," Kate complained to no one. Eyebrows went up. The remark served to make everyone more conscious of the room. It drove up sympathy for the woman as each one of them silently grocery-listed the snake's neglect of his wife and family. Stacey drew herself a picture of the shack: one room, a curtain over the left corner; likely the corner served as the parents' bedroom. In the right corner was a make-shift set of bunkbeds for the girls. Between them was the kitchen space. Above the stove were two shelves made of handcut rough cedar; to the right and left of the stove were two storage boxes. Little piles of brown bags, unmarked, housed tea, spices and what-not. Kate opened one bag and inside were three figurines, a kitten, a child and a woman.

"She must be Christian," Kate grumbled. "For all the good it does her."

"Kate," Momma snapped, "maybe you shouldn't be digging around Madeline's stuff like that." Kate ignored Momma's remark and just kept on digging into the little piles. She seemed to be trying to get some hint of what had happened here, as though the history of the moment were mysteriously locked into the piles of things tucked into the bags in disarray. Stacey had already started calculating what was missing in the house. There were no storage cupboards—everything was stored in plain view on two shelves or stuffed into two wooden crates to the right and left of the stove. No coat rack could be seen anywhere, no crocks to hold the flour, oatmeal and other drygoods safe from field mice invasion. A single lightbulb was the only electricity in the house.

"It's in what she doesn't have," Stacey whispered plaintively to Kate. Kate turned to look at Stacey; her large eyes seemed bigger in the shadow of dim light, almost innocent in their wondering what question Stacey thought she was answering. She stood still for a moment, then seemed to understand.

"Hmm," Kate agreed, finally understanding, and quit digging around. "There ain't much here, is there?" All three women looked intently at one another. "What could possibly drive the old snake to this level of neglect?" wanted to take shape, but none of them could find the words to ask the question.

Jim watched his aunt's every move. Eventually he reached into his pocket and took out a pouch of tobacco. Momma's brows knitted but she said nothing. Stacey looked at him full of surprise.

"Yeah," Ned said, "I will take a pinch myself." Pale blue smoke gently wafted in the air in long whisps. It curled about the yellow candlelight, fading into dark. It seemed to journey around their faces to the candles as though looking for the exit. Ella chuckled from her seat.

"Damn tobacco smoke looks as lost as we are." They all laughed at this. Stacey moved to stand next to Jim. She leaned on him; he put his arm around her without thinking. They stood like that for a few minutes.

"Stacey," Jim began, puffing at the last of his smoke, "I can't go back to that school. I don't know what it is but just now I can't stand them people. Do you think you could send me a book now and again?" It had been a long time since Jim had asked her to do anything for him. They had rarely spoken to each other this summer. It jarred her now in the midst of her mother's near-death to hear him ask for something so mundane as a book now and again.

"I would like to know something about these people before I die, but I just can't stand them," he continued, waving his hand at the scene before them. The old snake lay unconscious, fighting for his life. "Just can't stand them" had something to do with what had happened but no one seemed to be able to figure out what the connection was.

"Sure," she said absent-mindedly while she let her mind free-float, drawing up images without joggling them in any specific direction. "He's just like them," she uttered, her voice vacant of any emotion. They all nodded sagely. No one in this room liked him any more than they liked white folks in general. He hated his wife for the same reason any old white man could conjure—only he wasn't white. This made him pathetic. Saving him was as much a punishment as letting him die. He would go home to the same place as all their ancestors and would have to tell his entire lineage, his infinite grandmothers about the abuse he had heaped on Madeline and her children. He would spend all eternity weeping for his lost self, struggling for the redemption of his twisted spirit. His grandfathers would shun him and add loneliness to his pain. The wind would buffet him about aimlessly, screaming shame in his ear. Momma had just given him another chance to alter the text of his story before he left this world. She was absolutely convinced of their view of the other world. Although Stacey had her doubts about life after death, she decided to live her life as though there were another place in which your story had to be accounted for. No one alive could tell what happened to the dead, but to lead a decent lawful life, for whatever reason, couldn't hurt.

Madeline's breathing deepened. Stacey realized she had hardly been breathing all this time. As her breathing resumed depth her body relaxed and the distant look in her eyes came closer to the reality of the present. She came to her senses to pour out her story in flat, even tones. The snake had violated his daughter, his own daughter. Young Jim had to leave the room in the middle of the story, holding his hand over his mouth while his gut heaved. Ned followed him out the door. The rest of the women stood too shocked to react. No one else moved to help Jim. They all sat listening to the woman's tale, each of them feeling like they didn't really need to know this but unable to move away from the teller. She had sent her children away after that. She waited for the old snake to pass out, loaded up his gun, then waited for him to come to. One of the children had told the neighbour that her mother was going to shoot the old snake. The chief was sent for but he arrived at the moment of the execution of her plan.

"I couldn't even do dat right," she said. "He's still alive." A strange deep sound, almost inhuman, rose from her, filling the room with its nearly insane rage. Momma ran to Stacey, trying to get her out the door. Stacey refused to budge. Momma gave up. She moved to Madeline, breaking into a wailing song. Kate joined her, grabbing two pieces of firewood to act as drum. Soon the woman was singing her grief with them.

Stacey neither moved nor sang. The strength of Stacey's body leaked out in her silent thick moments of shock. Everything slowed down. The chief looked concerned, sad—sadder than he had ever looked. At the same time a look of absolute affection for Stacey warmed the sadness of his eyes. Soon he was singing, not to Madeline but to Stacey. Stacey lay down. Images without words, pictures of the epidemic, the drought-shrivelled mint, the spindly berries, the near-double-murder criss-crossed her mind, tripping over each other, sandwiched between the nameless thing the snake had done and Madeline's words, "I couldn't even do dat right." It was all too much. The weeping inside began again. Finally, Stacey joined them in song.

After the song, Momma gave Stacey something to make her sleep. Stacey dreamed of snakes all balled up, rolling out over the earth like pestilence. Snakes full of venom destroying everything in their path. Moving balls of hideous violations who sought everywhere for their victims, destroying them from within. Slime, filth and unease followed the snakes as they culled out the powerless, pulling them to their centre. In their innocence the victims' strength fell from their bodies the way Stacey's had just a few moments ago. The filth surrounded the people, got inside them, wrapped them in sheets of seductive walls. The people moved slower in the filth of the balls of snakes. Without energy they slept, woke only to plod through the rest of the day, returning to hovels of shame to sleep again. Stacey awoke in a terrible sweat. She wanted to recount her dream to someone but it seemed too bizarre, too hideous and far-fetched to have any real significance to their future, so she stayed quiet.

In her bed inside their house Celia awoke. She felt as though she was watching her sister dream. From inside the thin shaft of light which cut into their room from the kitchen, Celia watched the empty place where Stacey usually slept. The light misted, moved about, grew ghostly. Stacey's horror-filled face imaged itself up in the uninhabited place. Terrorized, Celia shrank deeply into her bed in the darkened room. Her skin felt as though something were creeping all over it. The creeping feeling wended its way toward her open, frightened mouth. She struggled to close it, shut her lips tight against this foreign feeling; her mouth would not obey. Sound wrapped in a ball of fear rose inside her stomach, jumped to the top of her belly, bounced against the canalway to her throat; then it, too, succumbed to defeat. Exhausted, she fell back upon the bed and slept.

After her fitful sleep Stacey awoke to Momma holding more tea. The Speaker and Ella had already arrived at an unprecedented decision: the woman and her children were to stay. They were already talking about the logistics of how all this would be worked out. She had no relatives to return to. The children were their children; the snake had to leave. The chief, the Speaker, Ella and the men of the house had left by the time Stacey came around. Only Momma and Madeline were left.

As Stacey struggled for enough consciousness to get ready to leave she repeated Madeline's name over and over—it kind of rolled easy off the tongue. Madeline, Madeline. . . Stacey pulled her socks and shoes on. . . Madeline, Madeline. . . while she donned her jacket. She turned to Madeline as she went out the door.

"Nice name." Madeline frowned, a little confused.

"Ay?" she asked.

"Your name," Stacey mumbled, "nice name." Momma and Stacey left.

CHAPTER

14

Time passed quickly for a short while, the mundane and the comic filling up the days. The village began moving again after the shock of the epidemic had settled. Children could now be seen climbing the tree in the centre of the village, swinging from its branches or scampering about the edges of the road day-dreaming or running about aimlessly by turns. Madeline had taken to coming over to Momma's at least once a day. She always brought some fluffy white breads with her which she called bannock.

Madeline was a woman of clockwork regularity; she always arrived just a few moments before breakfast, her daughters in tow. She visited for an hour or so, then went home. Stacey took to watching for her arrival. Madeline moved so gracefully, more rhythmically than did her own people. As soon as Madeline was within twenty feet of the house she broke into a toothy smile, like she was remembering the last joke they laughed at the day before. The two girls bolted into a run about the same time that Madeline smiled.

Madeline did not sit in a chair, she slid into it slowly. She had long thin arms and a tall narrow frame. Her face lacked cheeks. In their place stood high cheekbones and a chiselled-looking nose, long, slightly wider and straighter than white folks'. Her hair was fine and black, black, black, straight and long. Stacey realized one morning over tea that Madeline looked like the Indian she had once seen on a postcard in the store in town. Stacey remembered insisting on having it then; Momma had stubbornly refused.

In the middle of tea she left the house on the run, heading for the store. She had to get that card. On her return she showed it to Madeline, who laughed long and hard.

"Hell," she said, "every second Manitoba Saulteaux looks like dat." She laughed some more. "Never figured out how come dem people like our faces so much dey paint 'em." She shoved the picture aside to turn back to Momma. "Is it hard—dis fishin'?" Stacey held the picture, staring at Madeline. She couldn't stop. It was so remarkable to her. It dawned on her that Madeline's people must be the ones white people kept calling "exotic."

"So how come you bothered with the old snake?" Stacey interrupted. Momma gasped, her cup clattered to the table and she shot Stacey an ugly look which Stacey chose to ignore. Madeline's face went blank, then it looked hurt.

"It wasn't always bad," she whispered, her voice all swishy and husky. Momma recovered.

"This is none of your business, Stacey."

"I didn't mean it that way," Stacey defended herself. How had she meant it, she wondered? This Madeline whose name rolled around in the mouth long after you said it, whose legs swayed in time with some prairie breeze when she walked, whose cheeks weren't fat, had settled for some bandy-legged man, stalky, heavy-browed and almost brutish-looking compared to her. This Madeline, whose smile seemed to wake up the sun with its magnificence—who was so beautiful white men painted likenesses of her—had chosen such a man. What had she found so attractive in his short stout body? Madeline stared at her hands while Momma continued to glare at Stacey. Stacey wondered if the last series of thoughts she had were the ones she meant. She wasn't sure. Best to put the picture away and keep quiet.

"I didn't mean it that way," she repeated numbly and sat down. A hopelessness seized her. She felt as though nothing she could say would change the feelings she evoked in the women in the room. No words came to her to help her explain to them what she had meant. The words attached to her meaning inside failed to come forward even for herself.

Madeline chatted a little while longer, then left earlier than usual. The thickness in the room created by Stacey's remark never left until Madeline went out the door. Stacey wanted to say something to her before she vanished from sight. She couldn't. She watched through the window as Madeline strolled up the road. Her hips were a little stiffer, less rhythmic when she walked. Stacey felt as though she had knocked some of the grace from Madeline's walk. Before Momma spoke Stacey told her that there wasn't anything Momma could say that would make her feel worse than she felt just now.

The day unfolded between heavy sheets of self-recrimination. Stacey's mind danced between struggling to grab hold of what she really meant, imagining what Madeline thought she meant, and arguing with herself for thinking about the incident at all. Words are sacred, once spoken they cannot be retrieved. Sometimes they fall out of the mouth in moments of thoughtlessness when the speaker focusses on images which don't include the one spoken to, and burn holes in the lives of the listener. Stacey tried to dig up the words to clarify her thoughts but some dark patch kept clouding them, obscuring their meaning. This patch of dark didn't seem to have anything to do with Madeline or her strange union with the old snake. She was unwilling to dig around inside the dark material clouding her view of the meaning behind the words uttered to Madeline. This quarrel inside made the day drag. Every movement came laboured and slow. The frustration of having to beat back the cloth of her misunderstanding, struggle with the meaning of her words to Madeline, tired her. Finally, the day ended.

She didn't fall asleep right away. A blankness full of awake settled in. She stared at the empty unlit room, waiting for sleep to come to her. Her body was so still she barely breathed. Celia lay in the bed opposite wondering what strangeness had overcome her sister. The quiet was tangible. It had weight and occupied some strange space—a wall of soundlessness cocooned her sister, making the distance between them huge. As Celia drifted to sleep she was aware that this distance was slightly fearful to her. She made up her mind to leave early in the morning in case this change in Stacey was permanent.

The ordinary noises Stacey made in the conduct of her living held significance to her family, but no one noticed until she suddenly stopped making them. Momma cast worried looks in her direction all morning. Finally she asked what was wrong. Stacey had no answer that made any sense to her.

"Nothing." The trap door to understanding slapped shut. A wall of quiet came up between Momma and Stacey. There was no way out for Momma, so she accepted the void Stacey erected between them and carried on with the mundane business of living. Both grew dangerously quiet in the ministrations of their life; together, yet separate, they moved through the day's business. The rolls of thoughts which normally played about inside Stacey's mind all but stopped. The why of things which had coloured her character until now came to an abrupt halt—stopped dead by the obstacle she was too young to know could not be hurdled just now. She stopped herself from considering anything too deeply lest it come up to haunt her again.

Stacey's too-serious quiet diminished the joy in the house. It floated above the emotional being of the family, putting brakes on the natural unfolding of the family heart. The isolated presence of Stacey beleaguered the oneness of family, creating an unnamable pain for everyone. Celia took to leaving early and returning late. She hung about the village square looking for things to do which would keep her from going home. Celia had no idea that she was alienating herself from the family fold just as surely as was Stacey.

Finally, the day to leave for Yale was upon them. This time they would ride in Ned's car without having to hitch with some other relatives. Annie couln't go, Stella's little one was too small. Kate generally went in her own family's car. Momma agreed to fish for Annie if Stella's young man would come along. He showed up all ready to go.

The old snake had not recovered yet, but Ella was to have her way—he was ostracized. Meantime Madeline stayed at old Ella's. Annie and Momma still took turns taking care of the snake. The chief had already told him that, as soon as he was strong enough, he would have to leave. He made no objection. No one outside the two women nursing him dared to visit, not even to say goodbye. Momma and Annie cared for him without speaking to him or acknowledging his presence in any other way but to clean and dress his wound and ensure that food was available to him. Day after day he lay in the dark of his kitchen making no move to care for himself, waiting for the moment he was to leave. The villagers carried on with their lives without a twinge of conscience.

Ned fixed up a roof rack for his wagon. Stella's man and Young Jim were busy loading the rack when Madeline came swaying up the walkway, her young girls behind her. Stacey broke into a smile for the first time in a while. Celia got excited as she always did when she saw the two girls coming. The three of them trooped off at once.

"Don't go far," Momma said, throwing some urgency and seriousness into her voice as the three trundled off in the direction of the village hall.

"O.K.," they answered in unison, their high-pitched giggles punching at the morning air. Before Madeline shot the snake, the three of them had been reclusive. Stacey now knew it was because the old snake never let them out of the house. Each September the two girls had been sent to residential school, to be brought home again only during the summer. It was strange to see them up and about so freely day after day now.

As she stared at the receding backs of the girls Stacey thought about the old snake fathering them. He must have had some redeeming qualities because the girls were particularly lovely. They had the marvelously haunting look of their mother—the chiselled cheekbones, fine eyebrows—but their eyes were larger and half-mooned, like her own. They were taller than her relatives the same age, thinly built, yet promised to be heavy-chested like many of the women in the village tended to be.

Madeline called out to Momma, smiling as usual. Momma's jaw dropped. Madeline had no teeth.

"Where are your teeth?" she asked gasping, to which Madeline laughed.

"I had no teeth to begin with," she explained. She was having new ones made. The dentist told her to pick them up later this morning.

"How did you end up with no teeth—isn't everyone born with them?" Stacey asked. Both Momma and Madeline laughed at this question.

"The old snake knocked most of them out. Da rest jiss went bad," Madeline answered. Stacey froze. The snake had knocked out her teeth. She wanted him punished for it. Her face, how could he attack Madeline's glorious face. It was so public, so perverse to attack her face. Madeline paid no attention to Stacey's frozen look of shock.

"Came to wish you off," she said still smiling. Momma looked discomfitted by the toothless image of a smiling Madeline, but she tried harder to hide her response than did Stacey. They exchanged niceties for a while before Momma asked if Madeline had ever wanted to go fishing. Stacey wanted to groan. Momma was going to invite her and her children. The car would be crowded after all.

"Yeah. The old snake wouldn't take me dere," she said simply. The beginning of an invitation was on the table—Madeline wanted to go with them. The hint was out. Ned, Jim and Stella's man stopped packing to wait for Momma's response. Momma looked at Ned, who shrugged. It was up to Momma.

"Get your things together. We'll stop for your teeth on the way through town. We've plenty of room." Stacey wanted to laugh—there would not be plenty of room once everything and everyone was loaded into the old Ford. There would be three giggling girls, two young men, one older one, Momma, Stacey and Madeline all squeezed between the sleeping gear inside the car, with the fishing and camping gear all piled up on top. They would be stared at by white passers-by, a car-load of Indians in an old Ford wagon loaded to the hilt.

"Ella has to have fish too," Momma argued with no one. No one believed her, but pretending that Ella was the reason for taking Madeline along stopped Madeline from being grateful to Momma. The family knew Ella would have fish whether Madeline came or not. "'Sides, it'll be a way for Madeline to repay Ella for her kindness."

The night before Momma had gone on about how good it was going to be not to have to ride all the way to Yale in a crowded car with half a million kids hanging out the window. This morning she fixed it so that they were crowded. Stacey could handle paradox when it was good, but after Madeline left she teased Momma about not wanting to be crowded.

"Oh well," Momma said, enjoying the attention the teasing brought her, "wouldn't be fair if we were the only ones not jammed up tighter than a jar of fish." Madeline must have been sure Momma would invite her because it took her only five minutes to return with packs for herself and the girls. She got a little shy when everyone laughed at the speed of her return.

"Didn't take long to fill them packs," Ned chirruped and they all roared.

"Ella . . . " Madeline began, embarrassed. Stacey laughed with the others, looking at Madeline from under her heavy eyebrows. Madeline's face lost years in the joy of the family's affection. Her embarrassment took on the face of a shy teenaged girl; despite having no teeth, she looked lovely.

"The bus to Yale is now leaving," Ned announced, imitating the nasal-sounding voice of the only bus driver Stacey had ever heard. "All aboard" came out through his nose and the scramble to get in the car was on.

It is unbelievable how humans are, Stacey told herself halfway through the trip. We all eat at the same time, drink the same amount of water at the same time, but no one could coordinate the pit-stops. The ride to Yale jerked along with a stop every half-hour for the same reason but for different people. The body of human beings can be so incredibly inconsiderate. On top of it all, Madeline had a way of speaking that only Momma managed to get a handle on. Her speech was rapid, full of images which had no meaning to anyone in the car. She used animals from a scattered and flat prairie to describe her every thought, and she machine-gunned her words through some sort of accent no one was familiar with. That Momma understood anything she said surprised Stacey. When she returned from her pit-stop she assured everyone "my back teet ain'g flodin' no more," whatever that meant. Only Momma laughed.

Madeline was different in heavy doses. It took some getting

used to her sense of language, the presentation of her thoughts in her accent. She had an expressive way about her that was hard for Stacey to take. She was kind enough but she didn't have the same system of hinting the villagers abided by. Whatever she wanted she asked for, whatever she thought she said. She did whatever she wanted to as well.

Stacey was sitting under an old pine one morning watching Madeline, turning over and over in her mind how she was different. An old memory of grating camas root came back to her. She was five. Momma had asked her to grate the camas for the feast after the winter dances. Stacey hesitated, grated a little, then hesitated again. "What's wrong?" Momma asked. "Doesn't it hurt?" Stacey asked hesitantly. Momma had held her, then sat her down. "Yes, it does," she spoke softly. The melody of her voice changed. "Camas is here to take care of us. Never forget to be grateful. Don't waste her, remember she sacrifices her life to you. Whisper sweet words to her. Give her courage." Momma rocked Stacey back and forth.

Stacey felt like the camas root just now. On the one side, she found the wild abandon of Madeline attractive, energizing; on the other hand, the very wildness of her frightened Stacey. It stirred an unnamable desire inside. When Madeline was around she doubted the austerity she had been immersed in all her life. A sweet prairie dust-storm flitting about the hills did not seem sensible. The staidness of the mountains of Stacey's home, the powerful green, the giant cedars all called for a rigorous inner power, a discipline that she had accepted as the best possible form of human expression. Madeline was sensuous, she called up joyful memories of sun kissing skin, a light breeze cooling the hot kiss. She inspired the body to move gracefully, with full-blossomed passionate movement, greeting the world free of inhibition. It was annoying to have your whole self challenged so innocently.

This wild abandon and ill-discipline must have both attracted and enraged the old snake, Stacey decided. Madeline watched the work on the first day. The next day she chose whichever of the tasks appealed to her, whether or not the tasks were generally male or female, and she set to work. She dipped for fish, then hauled her catch up the hill, set it up to dry, then cooked for herself and anyone else who was "hungry enough to eat gophers," but she never cleaned a single dish. She did everything in a hurry. Her thin frame hid an inordinate amount of muscle power. The men were continually falling behind her. No one said anything to her about how women don't generally dip and haul fish—they clean them and dry them, then both men and women cook, after which the women wash dishes. She was gracious in an odd sort of way and her sayings inspired laughter once everyone got her accent down. There was a definite air of freedom about her. After a while no one but Stacey thought much about how different she was.

The two young girls were very much like their mother. Quieter than Madeline but equally industrious. Compared to the dogged pace of Stacey, Momma, Young Jim, Ned and Stella's man, these three were like whirlwinds determined to get through work as quickly as possible so they could get on with more fun things. For Stacey and her family the work itself was the only goal, the fun was somehow integrated into the labour process. Not so for Madeline and her girls. Not only did they choose the work they did but they did it with a vengeance. The work done, they gathered around Madeline as she pulled a funny little instrument from her skirt and they danced and sang the day away.

Magically, the frenzied pace of Madeline and her daughters stepped up the pace of Stacey and her family. The Madeline crew set out to catch and dry some forty fish a day. That done they kicked back to relax, tell stories and sing. Momma figured it wasn't such a bad way to do things, so she picked up her own pace. Ned and Jim followed Momma's example and Stacey fell in line. Stella's man alone continued to plod through the day, stopping with the others. They finished earlier each day until finally the fish were busy drying themselves in the wind with little for anyone to do but wait until they were dry.

Stacey read a story to her mom after breakfast on the first day off they had. Momma listened carefully for a time. She liked the story. She struggled hard to commit it to memory. After it was over, she asked Stacey how she could remember all of that in one blow. Stacey stared at her confused for a second, then laughed.

"I don't have to remember it, Momma. The words tell me what the story says." Now Momma was perplexed.

"So how do you know what the words are saying if you don't remember them?"

"Yeah," Madeline concurred, her voice rich with challenge. "How can you tell?" These words began Stacey's first class. She decided that the way she had learned wouldn't work for these women. They wanted to know now, not some five years down the road. She concocted a story about a family namd Alphabet, gave them names and work to do. She even threw in trickster behaviour for those moments when none of the Alphabets would do the right work. Madeline right away wanted to know why they had to do separate jobs and stick to them so rigidly. Stacey tried to explain conceptually what sort of confusion would arise if they all behaved any which way. Madeline didn't get it.

"Never mind, Madeline," Momma finally told her, "dey jiss do." Madeline giggled at Momma's imitation of her accent, agreeing to go along with the story.

"Crazy people, dem Alphabets."

"All anyone has to do is learn the jobs of each letter, then match up the sound they make at work with words they know." Stacey showed them a group of words. It was a sentence she had learned had all the letters of the alphabet in it.

"The quick brown fox jumps over the lazy dog," she said,

showing them each letter and carefully sounding them out.

"Should shoot dat dog," Madeline muttered.

"Madeline!" Stacey said stifling a laugh. "Mostly they behave pretty good, but every once in a while one of them takes it into their head to make a different noise—not too different, though, not so different that you can't tell what it's saying."

"I like dem letters best," Madeline said respectfully of the letters who jumped out of character occasionally. Everyone laughed. Pretty soon they were saying words and making Stacey spell them. Then Stacey would say words, making Momma and Madeline spell them. Finally, Stacey handed Momma the book, asking her to read the first line.

Momma scoffed. She knew the first sentence she said, she remembered the story. Stacey had forgotten about Momma's phenomenal memory. She flipped the pages to another story and asked her to read the line.

"Sus-san came home." Momma read aloud and everyone cheered her on. After she finished a page, Madeline grabbed the book and started to read. "She saw her husband dere on de couch." They all laughed excitedly. The reading was slow, jerky, and they stumbled over the unfamiliar and conundrums like "although," but by the end of the day the two women were reading. They could go everywhere all at once now; through books they could see the world and they felt the power of this new kind of vision.

"Got any of dem stories about China?" Madeline asked. "I always wanted to go dere."

"Yeah," Momma joined in assertively, "let's go to China." The two women squealed with delight. Ned wasn't too sure about this Madeline and the reading stuff. It was already changing Momma's modest personality. Reading might make a monster of her, he teased. Momma blushed but they pushed on. Stacey grabbed a history book from her bag of treasures and flipped through the pages until she came to the story of the Ming dynasty. They read until dark. Ned had to light the kerosene lamps. Stacey found it amazing that these two women responded so much alike to the words. The story of the dynasty, the wars, brought tears to their eyes despite the tempered and dull language it was framed in. They laughed at some of the attitudes it took to go to war in the first place, marvelling at the lack of heart of whoever had written this stuff who heroized the killers.

The next three days went like that, each moment filled with reading by the two women. Stacey gently guided them along, until finally the words took on easy familiarity. Stacey realized something too; it doesn't take that long to learn to read. Much of the time in class was spent in useless repetition, writing, rewriting and testing the students. If just reading were the goal of the schools no one would have to spend twelve years at it. This did not go by her mom either. On the third day she asked Stacey how come it took so long for her to learn to read. She told her mom that white kids don't remember things very well, so they had to have them repeat things year to year, day to day. The point was not so much reading as remembering what you had read.

"You'd think they would smarten up and remember," Momma chided.

"Must be the food they eat," Stacey said laughing. Momma agreed, but she didn't laugh. Instead she asked Stacey how come she didn't read out loud all the time. Stacey tried to persuade her mom that she could read silently. This was a difficult concept for her mom to grasp.

"How can you talk inside your mind?" They struggled with it for half a day before Momma clued in on what Stacey was trying to tell her. In desperation, Stacey resorted to their language, but that didn't work. Then she tried, "Dream it up as you see the words, envision the meaning," and Momma got it. Momma stared at the words in the book, then shook her head sadly.

"I hope the kids don't give you this much trouble, Stacey, but I just can't story it in my mind." Stacey wanted to laugh but checked herself.

"You still have to look at the words individually, Momma. You can't just stare at the whole works at once."

"Ohhh," she purred. After that it was considerably easier. She wanted to be tested too, just like the kids. Stacey tried to explain that the kids would not read such complex stories. Momma wanted to know why.

"Because they don't know as many words and the words they know don't hold the same meaning." Momma thought this out, then replied.

"I guess not. The 'flu means illness to them. For us it means terror." Everyone sat quiet. Madeline recounted her story of the 'flu. The old snake had gotten it and she had saved him. She was sorry now. She reached out, hugged her daughters close, falling silent under the gentle canopy of night. The kerosene lamp danced about, playing with the contours of her face, darkening it in places which accentuated the prominence of her cheekbones and the absence of flesh on the cheeks. The two girls leaned readily into their momma's arms. Stacey thought about how different this was. Momma occasionally fondled Stacey's hair but rarely did she hug her children.

After three weeks with Madeline, the girls and the books, change came to the family. Madeline was so effusive, it was contagious. She laughed hard and long, generally slapping whoever was near, not hard, but in a gentle familiar kind of way. She hugged her girls a lot. By the end of three weeks, Momma and Madeline took turns reading with one of the three girls on their laps or leaning up against the two women. Stacey liked this easy physical familiarity that Madeline was cultivating in her family. So did Ned. He had always been kind of physical himself. For him it was a happy transformation Madeline was bringing to the family. He sat with his arm about Young Jim, his hand resting on Momma's leg, listening to the nightly reading, peace and contentment written on his face.

The fish were finally dry, but no one really wanted to leave. Ned had begun dreaming of his union with Momma in earnest; mischievous thoughts pulled at him and his dreams of her plagued him. Momma was enjoying the rest so much and the others delighted in the joy which had been so fleeting since the days of the 'flu. Ned took things in hand. He was not a bossy man, his expectations of the women were small, but they all deserved the rest and the peace that floated about the camp for a little while longer.

He and Young Jim disappeared for a couple of hours. When they came back, Young Jim announced they would leave the day after tomorrow. Momma was about to protest, the huckleberries are ripe now. Jim had already considered this. They would all spend the rest of today and tomorrow picking the berries here at Yale. He was unsure about taking command this way. He posed this last remark like a question. Momma had veto power, both of them knew it. She assented. Jim told the kids, Madeline and Stacey they would all go ahead, Momma and Ned would come later. He had had to leer and wink at Madeline, which he hated doing, but it was the only way Madeline could be persuaded to go on ahead.

Stacey knew what was up. "Too much Raven," she laughed softly to herself. She picked up a pack to head for the hills. Madeline, Jim and the girls did the same. Stacey wondered how he had put his plan to Momma; likely she hadn't needed much convincing, the sanction of her son was probably enough.

On the hills overlooking Hell's Gate Canyon Stacey plucked away at the huckleberries. She was studiously filling her pack with berries, casting glances at the magical canyon below when she felt something on her nose. She twitched but kept picking. Plunk, another, she looked up. Young Jim was smiling all smug and proud.

"I told her culture and law is only good if it keeps people good-hearted and healthy." He laughed at the notion that Momma had bought that one. Stacey joined him. Momma had lost weight; with each pound gone her anxiety levels rose along with a burgeoning shortness of temper. Dark circles formed under her eyes from want of sleep; overwork and river baths weren't doing Ned much good either. In the hot hilltop sun, Stacey began to wonder when all this passion would be cut loose in herself. When would her body come alive over someone? She looked out over the hills, marvelling at the immensity of the land rolling out before them.

"Imagine, this is just a piece of her," she heard Young Jim whisper.

"I love you, Jim," Stacey answered. He grinned slyly back at her.

"Me too," he said. Stacey broke into a run after her brother. It didn't last long. He hollered back that she was going to jam her berries if she didn't quit.

Momma and Ned joined them that afternoon. They came up the hill holding hands, speaking softly, smiling at the lot of them. The two slept in the same tent that night without pretence of waiting any longer. Stacey smiled just before she rolled into her dreams.

CHAPTER

15

IF ANYONE IN THE VILLAGE DISLIKED THE IDEA OF NED moving in so soon after old Jim's departure no one said it. Village life resumed its pace without any hint of its feelings about Ned taking up with Momma. Stacey supposed it was because they decided it was inevitable, Momma being how she was and all. No one could have guessed that they just couldn't care anymore. They were tired, not the easy tired of a long day's work, but overcome with the deep fatigue of losing battle after battle on the trail to clan survival.

The old snake left sometime during their fishing time, so Madeline moved home again. Annie described his departure. He had stood upright like soldiers do. The villagers lined the path to witness his departure. The snake struggled with his lost dignity, waving to each of them. No one responded. At the bridge he turned a sharp about-face, gave one last wave. The villagers stood, eyes straight forward, waiting for him to cross the bridge. Momma listened to the story, heaved a sigh, then asked Annie if she wanted more tea. A chill went up the spine of young Celia. The snake left without a goodbye from anyone. Have some tea, Annie, Celia muttered to herself, shivering one more time.

Madeline moved back to her house. She dropped off a half-hundred dried fish with Ella, then took her half of the huckleberries. Stacey thought this generosity had more to do with Madeline's indifference about the fruit rather then her affection for Ella. As is sometimes the case with cynical thoughts, Stacey was wrong. Madeline loved the delightful berries so well that after a couple of days she came by to see if the berries grew around the village as well. Momma offered to show her where. The next morning she and Madeline rounded up the village kids and the bunch of them headed up the hill. Stacey was glad she was wrong. She decided not to speculate on anyone's motivation without a fairer hearing than she had given Madeline. Not that it hurt Madeline at all; no one knew she had entertained doubts about her.

Stacey was still curious about what Steve had had to say about Polly, but it was clear he wasn't going to come by her house anymore. He had kept up his periodic visits with Ella though, and one afternoon Stacey could see him over at her house. She wondered what sort of stories Ella had to tell him, while she mentally calculated what to bring over to Ella's—not a good idea to go to an old woman's house for counsel empty-handed during harvest season. Ella probably had no jarred fish since few of the villagers except Momma, courtesy of Ned, had canners. Probably the jarred fish would be easier for her to eat than the *shtwhen*. She packed up a half-dozen or so jars, loading them into the same brown bag she had gotten from her aunt. They looked so lonely in the big bag, she added another half-dozen jars. Stacey had no right to help herself to Momma's fish this way, they weren't hers to parcel out like this. She decided Momma would understand and left.

Steve had brought Ella something too. He was showing her a

pair of fold-up canvas wooden chairs. Ella seemed to like the invention. They were so light, delicate-looking, yet they managed to hold up her ample body. How smart some white folks are, Ella mentioned as she harrumphed up and down in the sturdy little chair. Steve confessed that the white men who sold them got the idea from someone else. This Ella found even more amusing.

"So they even steal ideas," Stacey could hear her quip. She and Steve laughed. He must know her well, Stacey told herself, to be able to laugh at his own like that. Ella looked up at her first. She started right in on the story of the magic chairs Steve had brought. Stacey smiled, giving her the fish. As usual, Ella was overjoyed by the fish, behaving as though Stacey were the most considerate human being in the world. No wonder everyone presented her with gifts—she was such a gracious recipient. Stacey smiled, sitting down. Ella got up and excused herself right away saying she had been tired a lot lately. Stacey didn't believe her. Ella was being polite.

"Try the chair, child, try the chair," she said before disappearing into her house.

"It's been a while," Steve offered carefully. He still dreamed of her. He had taken Ella's advice reluctantly. "Leave her alone until she finishes this UBC," old Ella had said. "You white people think so much of yourself. Everything is so easy for you. Not so for the rest of the world. She won't finish if you don't leave her be. It isn't just her who will suffer. See all the little ones here. They are her relatives. We don't feel the same about relatives, you and I. . . ." Her voice had a kind of urgency, an intensity, almost a warning in it. It had held Steve still and quiet for a long time. He remembered almost word for word the content of Ella's plea. Now Stacey was here. The words held him in check.

Stacey tried out the chair, asking him where he got them. He recited the history of the chair. Some place called Indonesia used them. Some white men saw them, patented them, built them and sold them.

"So that's what Ella was saying—they even steal ideas." Stacey laughed. Steve did too. He launched into a long discussion about other ideas someone had scooped and patented and gotten rich from. Stacey wondered how they managed to shamelessly steal the thinking of so many different people whom they called inferior. When Steve stopped talking she said this aloud.

"I don't know," he answered, curious. "I never thought about it before." This surprised Stacey. It made her wonder what else he did not have to think about. How much of the information he owned inspired thoughts in him, how much just gets filed in his mind without him ever thinking about it again? She tried to gauge by looking at him how serious a thinker he was; it was hard to tell.

"Do you ever think about Polly?" she asked. Steve sat down, folding his hands in his lap. He asked her why she was so obsessed with Polly.

"Why are you so callous about her?" she retorted.

"Well, it isn't like you two were fast buddies. I never once saw you speak to each other." There was a thin-sounding edge to his voice, a smugness. It snipped at Stacey's insides, quick and razor sharp. He looked sorry he had made that last remark. She ignored the slice his words made, reminding him of what he had said a long time back, "You said it wasn't just the note."

"Her dad was an alcoholic, beat both Polly and her mom regular . . ."

"And women can't get divorced," Stacey put in for him. "Maybe she had no family, no one to stand by her," Stacey added.

"Maybe no place in society," he ventured. He trod on foreign territory here in putting things this way. Stacey was not familiar with his standard radical sociological language, but she didn't seem to have trouble grasping the concept of "no place." What he didn't realize was that for Stacey no family and no place were synonymous. After a while he laughed.

"What's funny?" Stacey asked.

"Well, every other person I talk to thinks my thinking is fairly crazy. You don't seem to."

"Don't be too sure," she teased. They arrived at some sort of understanding Stacey thought she could work with. Polly was becoming tangible, understandable, less confusing. Stacey felt she had enough of a picture to sort the rest of her story out. The evening was falling about them everywhere, semi-light and shadow dark, the night blossomed. It was almost time to retreat to her room. Steve looked a little antsy so she stayed seated for a bit.

"Is it because I am white?" he asked without bothering with the first part of the question.

"No," she said softly, "it's because you aren't Indian." She couldn't sort out the difference between these two approaches clearly enough to explain, so she just rose to leave. He reached into his pocket, pulling out a pack of cigarettes.

"Give me one of those," she said. They both pulled hard on the smokes.

"There is this gulf between us. I have no idea how deep or wide it is. I just know it's there. I don't know if any two people can bridge it. It may take something more." She stared at the coming night for a moment, sighed then finished. "Hell, I don't even know if I even want it bridged." She realized that there was something mercurial, almost mystical, about her obsession with attending university—something which had nothing to do with teaching her younger villagers. It had more to do with coming to grips with the why of his world without the understanding having any pragmatic destiny. She just wanted to know. He in the meantime had no context for seeing her as she really was, judging whether or not she was likeable. Without context, any relationship is doomed, she decided, pulling on the smoke again. Context, she knew, kindles the smouldering embers which bind family together.

"No context, Steve. There is no context for you and I."

"I have been talking to Ella," he argued defensively.

"And you can do so for the rest of your days, but until you have experienced the horror of an epidemic, a fire, drought and the absolute threat these things pose to the whole village's survival— and care about it, care desperately—you will be without a relevant context."

"I can't conjure that up in my side of town," he sulked.

"How did it feel to watch us die, Steve?" she asked. It was mean. She didn't care much that it was mean. Steve blushed. His father was one of the white doctors who could not possibly be expected to cross the river to treat "those" people. He had so easily persuaded his son of the interests of his patients, his workload . . .

"I . . . I . . ." Steve stammered.

"Don't know what to say, Steve?" Stacey flicked her smoke out on the ground in front of her. "Shame, Steve. You are now feeling shame," she said without any emotion whatsoever.

Steve was uncomfortable with his shame, unlike the old snake, who had packed his things with serious deliberation as though he were about to embark upon a great adventure. He marched upright through the village, his whole personage behaved as though all the people who had gathered were there to see him off. At the arc of the bridge he had turned to wave, no one waved back. Even this lack of response had not bent his shoulders the way Steve's now curved. Stacey knew the old snake felt deep shame. Shame so deep he had not defended himself. Shame so deep he left quietly as soon as he was able to walk. His assumption of dignity was to assure the people he had no quarrel with their decision. He had not wished to add the coercive force of guilt on top of his crime against womanhood onto the shoulders of the community.

Steve's bent shoulders culled a twinge of guilt inside Stacey. She tried to shake it off. The gulf between them widened. It grew until it became an ugly maw. A maw filled with a powerful raging wind that whirled everything into its centre. Stacey hung fast to the fragile thread of herself. This maw could swallow her, given the opportunity. She resisted the pull of the wind.

Finally Steve left. She watched his lonely defeated back, feeling sorry for the whole of white town for the first time. White town had no other story but its own. No Raven, just ratty tatty old crows. Crows who cawed noisily, hungrily arguing for recognition from the settlers of the town. Crows whose feathers were always askew. Crows without dignity. Crows whose lack of dignity stood in the way of even the most modest transformation.

She realized white town was a still town. Nothing moved. There was no perceptible rhythm in the hum of white town's business, just an ache and a deep emptiness. It was why the good Owenite doctor, Steve's father, could argue against his own oath to humanity and not come to the village. Despite his sociological radicalism, his intellectual recognition of racial equality, he could translate patients into cash income—sustenance without conscience. He could translate her village into a squalid hopeless condition in his mind. He had patients he had to treat. He could save them.

As Steve reached the bridge Stacey finished her imagined story of him. He had designs on society. Designs which would bear fruit. He carried his future in his approach to life. He segmented the world in his heart, divided it up piece by piece, arranging it all in a neat stack of feelings, from the close feelings one has for family to a distant coolness for the rest of the world. He did not confuse this segmentation with heartfelt compassion, but rather calculated the quantity of heart he needed to get by wherever he stood. In the village, he added greater humour to his usual quiet seriousness. He got by. In the end, Stacey decided he was not enough for her.

"Too much Raven," she said aloud, laughing at the curved figure of Steve as he disappeared behind the arc of the bridge. The sun had been shining hot again. The road was dry. Stacey felt the future in a way she had not felt it before. The door to this future was open, the view hazy, but that didn't matter. Steve's future was pre-cut from some cloth she did not want to wear. His back reminded her of Polly. It no longer mattered why she killed herself.

A crow stopped mid-flight, landing just feet from where she stood. Her muscles tightened, hardened. Crow strutted back and forth in front of Stacey. Stacey laughed.

"It's attitude, Raven—attitude."

Stacey returned to the house. It was filled with people who, anticipating the loss of Stacey, came by to visit. The sound brought contentment with it. Celia seemed different. Rather than play about the kitchen with Madeline's girls or run about outside, she busied herself padding after Stacey. She had this bouncy determined walk that was like Young Jim's, too grown-up for her years. It almost made Stacey laugh. Momma seemed to sense what Stacey was thinking because later that night she told Stacey about how she was just like Celia when she was little. Stacey's memories had never been self-focussed. She remembered things well, but not usually things about herself. They didn't seem all that important. Momma sometimes talked about the past, but this was the first time she had ever talked about what Stacey had been like as a child. There was no lesson to be garnered from it. The teaching of this one slid by Stacey.

Stacey and Celia fell into a rhythm behind Momma. Even during a drought summer was a flurry of food-gathering and preservation. Momma, Stacey, Celia and whichever other kids weren't busy took to the hills at daybreak with Stacey's Gramma's berry-baskets strapped to their backs. It took them twice the time to pick half the berries, but it didn't seem to matter. Momma was always fun to be with during Stacey's last days at home.

"One time," Momma began one evening while they all gathered around to clean the fruit of twigs and bugs, "Gramma took us up the hill, just like today, sun spilling healing light down mercilessly. Oh, she was a hot one. We didn't tell Gramma, but her skirt picked up a lot of twigs. You know she wears them long kinds full of cloth. Old Gramp must've made money with that old logging outfit, one time, because Gramma always had a lot of cloth in her skirts. Had a lot of skirts too.

"Well, we're just picking away and we hear this grunt. Gramma says, 'Jacob, you quit your complaining and keep on picking. Never seen such a boy. He eats plenty and harvests little.' Annie tugs at Gramma's skirt. Gramma looks down. *'Ta'ah,'* she says, 'Jacob ditn't cum wif us.' Gramma looks up and there's this big ol' bear standing there. Just on the other side of the bush. Gramma hoists up her skirt, removes her fish knife from her leg strap and starts yelling at that bear. 'What you doing here, you don't belong here, your patch is that way, now get on with you.' The darn thing took off, too." The kids all laughed at the image of their tiny Gramma just a-hollering at a big old bear.

"Well, Gramma was a little vain. When she was young, all the boys thought she was just the prettiest sweetest woman. She hung onto this picture of herself forever. Soon as the bear is gone she looks at her skirt, then cuffs me. 'How long you been staring at these twigs knowing I look a mess?' Me, I just keep on picking. No sense defending yourself when you're caught red-handed. Gramma wouldn't give up. 'How long?' 'About since they got there, Momma.' I was so bad. I laughed. Gramma did too when she remembered we were the only ones on that hill anyway."

Stacey looked at Momma's face. A few whisps of grey danced about ahead of all the black. There were no lines on her face. Her face was indescribably sweet—the sweetness made her look much younger than she was. Stacey wondered what Momma thought about her own face. Probably didn't think about it at all, she decided. The village put no coercive store in a woman's beauty.

Here being a good woman yielded greater rewards then being beautiful. Momma thought about being a good woman a lot, but not at all about how she looked to others.

Stacey's last day ended gloriously. Light clouds lined distant hills and the sun painted gold, red and magenta streaks across her path as she faded out of sight. The clouds were so piteously thin they seemed to whisper a private plea to those below to help fatten them up. Young Jim looked up before offering his first bit of tobacco to the glory of earth, uttering his hopes for tomorrow. It was the last time for a long time that anyone in the village would offer tobacco, but Stacey could not know that.

Madeline came along behind them as they all made their way down the hill. She sounded like she was humming a tune. Stacey tried to name the music in her mind. She couldn't. It was foreign, the strains of it high-pitched, not low or wilful like her own music. It sounded painfully tender, beautiful yet plaintive and yearning. Stacey wanted her to sing louder, but she knew better than to ask. They made it down the hill just as dark closed in on them.

In the dark on the eve of Stacey's departure the rain came again. She came softly at first, a woman weeping, delighted at her ability to shed tears at last for her lost children. She wept steadily through the night, gathering strength. She wept long for the lost ones. She gathered her grief in dark clouds of rebirth, her tears slashed small gashes across the land where the earth dipped. She filled the creeks with tears for the pall that had wandered into the village in the wake of the 'flu.

Earth knew, just as Raven knew, that this was not the last epidemic. One more—the village would have to come through one more before the children could begin to talk to the others. Right now they had no idea what needed to be said to fill the gulf Stacey saw. Earth wept for the waning strength of the village, the great dreams of young Stacey and the dashing her dreams would take before Raven could return. Her spirit retreated to deep sobbing for the innocence of the villagers, an innocence the next generation would have to give up. There was no other way, Raven had decided. Both the earth and Raven knew all the people belonged to them. Raven could never again be understood outside the context of the others.

Before the others came, Raven lived in these small villages scattered far and wide. Far away the earth bled, her bleeding becoming an ulcer. Century by century, the ulcer intensified. It grew more serious millennium by millennium, until neither earth nor Raven had any choice. "Bring them here to Raven's shore. Transform their ways. Deliver Raven to the whole earth." That was the plan, but the villagers had resisted these people who had behaved even worse than first anticipated.

They gobbled up the land, stole women, spread sickness everywhere, then horded the precious medicine which could heal the sickness. With each sickness the silence of the villagers grew. The silence grew fat, obese. It had taken Raven almost a century to drive the people from the village, still the villagers would not communicate with the others. Epidemic after epidemic had not birthed the shame Raven had hoped for among the people of white town, so the villagers remained staunch in their silence. It was not until this last 'flu epidemic that finally the seeds of shame were sewn. Raven grew excited. Stacey had been the one to sew this seed in the heart of young Steve. Stacey didn't know this but it didn't matter to Raven . . . soon . . . soon . . . she could return.

The earth wept for the tragedy that would next befall the villagers. She knew there was no other way for them to understand white town without this next change. Until the villagers began to feel as ugly inside as the others, none could come forward to undo the sickness which rooted the others to their own ugliness.

Stacey's sleep was fitful. She tossed and turned through the night. Even in sleep she hesitated to leave. She doubted for a moment the value of her departure. Raven panicked. Raven brought

Gramma's voice to Stacey's ears: "We will never escape sickness until we learn how it is we are to live with these people. We will always die until the mystery of their being is altered." The words were not comforting but they firmed up Stacey's resolve to leave.

Stacey awoke to the sound of heavy rain. Serious rain. Rain that would end the cursed drought. The sound of rain strengthened her vision of the future. It did not matter to her that her vision was cut from a confused cloth, a cloth made of disparate threads from her past warped alongside the threads of white town, with unknown threads waiting to be shuttled overtop. Stacey awoke resolute. She would go forth, collect the magic words of white town and bring them home. She would try to bring them home in a way that would revitalize her flagging community. This was enough for earth and Raven.

In the morning half the villagers gathered to see her off. Momma, who had prepared enough food for the whole village, was disappointed, but she said nothing. Stacey for some reason had insisted on streamers—skinny bits of coloured stretchy paper that served no use had to be hung all over the place. It made no sense to Momma but she hung them up without complaint.

Ella showed up with Madeline and her girls. They were now becoming familiar to everyone. The girls had a number of friends among the village children besides Celia. Even Young Jim chatted with them in a friendly way. Momma still referred to her as the snake's woman, which annoyed Stacey more than it did Madeline. When Stacey asked her if she minded, Madeline shrugged, "No one calls Momma by her name." This took Stacey aback. It was true. Stacey didn't even know her Momma's name. She wanted to ask Momma about it but the question seemed too intimate to ask amid the comings and goings and the bits of conversation of the villagers. She chuckled to herself before letting the thought go: she'd been called Momma for so long probably no one remembered her real name.

Just then Steve came strolling down the path all alone. Ella greeted him at the door. Momma grumbled something about "don't know what old Ella sees in that boy." Stacey raised her eyebrows at Momma's indiscretion. Momma shot her a threatening look. Stacey backed down. The epidemic had made Momma steely in her unforgiveness of these people. They had watched the villagers die. One day they would all pay for watching a people die. Stacey knew it was unforgivable. She saw the fire in her mind, remembering that even the old snake had rolled out of his hut to organize their resistance to it. During their fight with the 'flu the old snake had sacrificed some of his alcohol toward the healing of the villagers. In a crisis everyone pitched in. Not so with these people. They moved about their lives, mowed their lawns, weeded their gardens as though the fate of life outside their matchbox homes had nothing to do with them. Still, Stacey thought Momma was awfully hard on them.

"They aren't human," she had told Stacey a while back, categorically dismissing them all. Momma took a look around the room at the streamers and doubts about the wisdom of sending Stacey out to learn to be like them took shape. She shrugged. She would have to trust Stacey to understand her laws and hope—hope the Raven spirit that snapped behind Stacey's eyes would not be culled out of her by their inhumanity.

The day was becoming a challenge for Stacey, who struggled to finish packing amid the confusion of people who plied at her for one last moment of attention while she hustled to pack on time for the bus. Each one who came to wish her farewell had some small advice to give her. Not one would be hurried in having their say. Stacey's frustration level rose. Her frustration sat open on her face. Momma shot her a warning look, one last look warning her to behave. There would be no more looks after this. Stacey would come back a woman beyond her mother's reach. Rena, alone, stood off to the side, not wishing to interfere with Stacey's efforts to leave. German Judy was not there.

"Where's Judy?" she asked.

"You know Momma has no more use for them people." No more words were said. Stacey was sad, but then she remembered Momma's words: "she's white and and so she doesn't count." This time Polly did not come into view. Instead, Nora, bold and unapologetic, strode into her imagination: "Momma is neither wrong nor right. Of course they count, but not right now." Nora receded. Stacey's eyes widened, then she sucked in air. Later. Everything seemed too big for today. Stacey closed the last of her clothes into the tattered suitcase German Judy had sent over with Rena. Stacey almost decided that she shouldn't be so crass as to use it since German Judy did not feel welcome in Momma's house. She shrugged it off. She needed something to put her clothes in, so she snapped it shut.

She looked up to see Rena leaning against the doorway to her room, alone. Stacey stared for a second, then strode in her direction. "I need a smoke," she said. Rena smiled. They grabbed Young Jim on the way out. They stood smoking, staring intently at one another, all the while Rena had a funny half-smile on her face, like she knew something and was just waiting for Stacey to ask her what's up. Stacey wasn't even curious. She was too busy savouring this one last quiet smoke with Rena and Jim. The wordlessness of the moment was full of reverence, of anticipated loneliness, yet Stacey felt well loved. The intensity thinned. Jim murmured "Don't forget my books." They laughed. Comic relief. Finally Rena nodded in the direction of the house, signalling Stacey it was time to go; no words, no goodbyes and no promises were exchanged, just the gesture of a comfortable moment smoking together. Stacey had the feeling that coming home would be so good after she finished university. Somehow Rena's ceremonial smoke with her had birthed the feeling.

It was time to go. Momma insisted they walk over the bridge

together—alone. Ned wanted to drive them in the car.

"Pick us up at the bridge," Momma ordered. Ned shrugged. Momma struggled with the suitcase, despite Stacey's protest. "It is the last thing I will ever do for you," she muttered, clinging to the case. "After this we will do things together, but not as mother and child." Her voice was casual, but her body was tense, full of her heart. Stacey felt like crying. She felt like letting the water run from her eyes as shamelessly as the earth let go rain. Something inside her made her swallow it back. To cry over the fact that she was leaving a child and would return a woman seemed so silly after all the deaths from the 'flu and the prospect of another hard winter created by the drought.

At the bridge Momma stared at her. She put the suitcase down carefully just like the men who had lowered Gramma into her grave had done. Something is dying here, Stacey thought, then pushed it out of her mind. Momma touched both sides of Stacey's face. Stacey swallowed. The rain poured over the two women, hiding the tears sneaking out from both their eyes. Then, like Madeline, Momma grabbed Stacey, holding her tight. It had been so long since her momma hugged her that Stacey's body convulsed with the meaning of the embrace.

"Momma," she whispered hoarsely into her mother's shoulder, "I don't know your name." Momma bent double with laughter so suddenly Stacey resented it.

"Momma is my name." She laughed so hard the words were hardly intelligible. She recovered enough to finish. "It was the first word your Gramma learned. She thought it was a name. Imagine having Momma for a name." Both broke into hysterics. "If I'd stayed in school, them nuns would have changed it."

Stacey took one last look at the landscape of her home. Despite the rain, the river was still shrivelled to a thin stream. White town glared at them from beyond the bridge, sterile white homes with bright colourful trims, roofs all in full repair. Automobiles trundled apathetically along the road, music from one or two of them wafted out the windows and hung about the women reluctant to move on. Down the side of the road to town was a concrete sidewalk. It was the only road in town which boasted such a thing. Stacey had watched the men working in the hot sun building it. They were planning to build more of the miserably hard things. Soon there would be no earth under their feet in town.

The picture of white town stood incongruous with the village. Behind the women stood the homes of people so familiar to them that no questions about their lives were ever exchanged. Ahead lay a land of strangeness—a crew of sharp-voiced people almost unintelligible to the people behind them. Momma's faced softened, grew concerned. "Must be something awful goes on behind their doors to make that girl kill herself like that," she said.

They turned simultaneously to wave Ned forward. A half-dozen cousins ran alongside the car. Inside, Celia, Young Jim, Auntie Annie, Kate and Stella had somehow managed to squeeze into the back seats. Stacey and Momma took up the seat in front like royalty. The cousins running alongside stopped when the car did. Momma waved them in.

The town stared at the car-load of kids that drove slowly down the street. They all looked at Stacey and her family as though no one in that car belonged in this here respectable old town. No one in the car cared. Stacey was to be sent off by as many people as the old wagon would hold.

No tears were shed at the depot. It was odd. It was as though the epidemic had created a drought in their hearts. They had been bled dry of tears. A distance small and almost invisible stood between each one of them. They were an exhausted raggedy family now. No one saw it clearly, but it was there even then. Stacey got on the bus and waved. That was it.

E P I L O G U E

"T HAT WAS 1954," STACEY HEARD HERSELF SAY SOME
twenty-five years later. "It was the last epidemic we fought as a
community. The world floated in, covering us in paralysing
silence and over the next decade the village fell apart. Women left
to marry after that. They left in droves. No one knows why; it was
as though the whole consciousness of the village changed at the
same moment. The women lost the safety of family. The village
lost its clan base because of it. Now we are caught in an epidemic
of our own making and we have no idea how to fight it."

The story had begun as an answer to her son's question, "Why
did little Jimmy shoot himself?" Her nephew had shot himself.
The dilemma of Polly had revisited Stacey. In trying to answer the
question with a story she felt the necessity to recapture the lost
sense of community that lay wounded in the shape of Jimmy's suicide. It took all winter for Celia, Stacey, Momma and Rena to recount that summer. Young Jacob sat in silence listening to the
women.

"In the end, they would not let us build our school. No one in white town would hire me either." She threw her hands up into the air. There was nothing else left to tell. "Not allowed" seemed to be all there was left to their life.

"Why did anyone pay attention to them?" The question was innocent enough. Why had they? The women stared at Jacob, horrified by its innocent simplicity. Celia stared at the box her son lay in. Why? She wondered what his children would have looked like. How many children would he have had—three, four? Horror pushed itself up. She could not stop recounting the numbers of dead babies from epidemic after epidemic and multiplying the numbers of children those babies would have had: 1840—100 dead childless children, smallpox. 1885—37 dead childless children, diptheria. 1905—57 dead childless children, measles. . . A sound came up—ravensong, powerful almost inhuman. . . 1918 —93 dead childless children, influenza. Memory after memory pushed up the sound. She imagined the faces of the babies these children might have had and she calculated their numbers. 1920—1940 tuberculosis, 157 dead childless children.

The numbers grew staggering. The great-great-grandchildren the village should still have, the great-grandchildren, their grandchildren, their children. Whole lineages wiped out. Hundreds became thousands. The loss filled the sound of grief. The grief shook the walls, rattled the women, terrified young Jacob. Momma raced from the room, dug about in her trunk and retrieved an old hand drum. She reached inside herself for the strains of their ancient grieving song. Rena, Stacey and Celia joined in wailing the song, expunging the old grief from their insides. The question still hung in the air when the song was over. Relieved of their grief, the women laughed.

"Why did we pay attention to them, of all people?" Rena repeated.

"Not enough Raven," Stacey answered. They laughed some

more. Jacob wasn't sure what wheels he had turned in the women's minds but he knew the story was not over. He wanted to know how "not enough Raven" had decided their fate. His lips drew into a faint pout. Celia laughed at his pout. She knew Stacey had answered the question. She also knew it would take Jacob some time to unravel the answer.

"Don't worry son. You'll know the answer when you need to."

CHARMAINE PEEL

LEE MARACLE is the author of *I Am Woman* (1988), a unique blend of storytelling, autobiography and poetry; *Bobbi Lee: Indian Rebel*, an auto-biography of her early years, published in 1975 and revised and reissued in 1990; *Sojourner's Truth and other stories* (1990), a spirited collection of stories, and *Sundogs* (1992), her first novel. Her essays, poems and stories have been published in numerous anthologies and journals, and she is also co-editor of *Telling It: Women and Language Across Cultures* (1990). Lee was recently awarded a Canada Council creative writing grant and is working on her next book.

MARIANNE NICHOLSON is an artist of Native descent. She uses photography as a mechanism to deconstruct the representations of Native peoples. Her work attempts to break down stereotypes and to develop an imagery that reflects both the traditional and the contemporary.

PRESS GANG PUBLISHERS FEMINIST CO-OPERATIVE is committed to producing quality books with social, literary and feminist merit. We prioritize Canadian women's work and include writing by lesbians and by women from diverse cultural and class backgrounds. Our list features vital and provocative fiction, poetry and non-fiction.

A free catalogue is available from: Press Gang Publishers 101—225 East 17th Avenue, Vancouver, B.C. v5v 1a6 Canada